Jimmy Zest

Jimmy Zest is an inventor. Nobody knows what he will dream up next – but everyone knows it's likely to be trouble.

A marvellously funny collection of stories about Jimmy – not to mention his friends, Gowso, Penny Brown, Knuckles, Shorty and Legweak.

First published in 1982
by Hamish Hamilton Children's Books
This Magnet edition published 1984
by Methuen Children's Books Ltd
11 New Fetter Lane, London EC4P 4EE
Text copyright © 1982 Sam McBratney
Illustrations copyright © 1982 Thelma Lambert
Printed in Great Britain by
Richard Clay (The Chaucer Press) Ltd,
Bungay, Suffolk

ISBN 0 416 50130 3

Jimmy Zest

SAM McBRATNEY

Illustrated by Thelma Lambert

A Magnet Book

Contents

1
Jimmy Zest's Egg Box Wonder

ONCE Jimmy Zest started collecting egg boxes it became a habit.

This is the sort of thing that he did. When his mum came back from the shops he met her at the door to help her carry in the parcels. In the kitchen his mum stood on a stool and Jimmy Zest reached her stuff out of the parcels to put it into the cupboards — sugar, baked beans, biscuits — all that sort of thing.

"Huh," said Jimmy Zest, "didn't you get any eggs?"

His mum looked down at him from a great height.

"I got eggs yesterday," she said, not a bit pleased. "Do you want this family eating eggs until we've all turned into chickens? Eggs, eggs, eggs."

Jimmy Zest did not want eggs, eggs, eggs. He wanted boxes, boxes, boxes.

One day — it was a Saturday — he got his mum into big trouble in the supermarket.

The supermarket was a huge place, the kind of place some children got lost in. But Jimmy Zest knew how to look after himself. And he knew where they kept their eggs.

The egg shelf was always packed full with beautiful boxes. They had grey boxes, pink boxes, cardboard egg boxes, plastic egg boxes. There was only one thing wrong with them. They had eggs in them.

On this particular Saturday, Jimmy Zest didn't let that stop him. While his mum was at the cheese counter, he filled a plastic shopping bag with egg boxes.

Nobody saw him — or so he thought. When they got to the checkout the woman at the till pointed at his plastic bag and said to his mum, "Is there anything in that bag? What has he got in that bag?"

Jimmy Zest slid the bag round the back of his legs to hide it.

"Oh, it's just meat," his mum said nicely. "It's already paid for."

By this time there was a man standing beside them. Jimmy Zest did not like the look of him. He was bald and fierce.

"I'm afraid there's more than meat in *that* bag,

madam," he said, as he scratched his head with one finger.

So there was, of course. One look at the face of Jimmy Zest told all. There might just as well have been a sign round his neck saying: THIEF.

"What have you got in that bag?" his mum snapped at him.

The bald man bent down and opened it.

"It's full of eggs," he declared.

"It's not," said Jimmy Zest.

"Oh but it *is*," the man said, showing an angry mouthful of twisted teeth.

Jimmy Zest led them all the way back to the egg shelf, where he stopped and pointed at three dozen brown eggs, all out of their boxes.

"Those are eggs without boxes," said Jimmy Zest. "In here, in my bag, I've got boxes without eggs."

His mum stood with her mouth open, waiting for words to happen.

"Oh! You little . . . wart! Oh!" She turned to the bald man. "*You* talk to him. Tell him you'll put him in jail."

The man was scratching his head again, just where the hair started.

"Well, I don't think we could put him in jail,

exactly. If he'd taken the eggs and left the boxes — that might have been different."

"I don't want eggs," said Jimmy Zest. "Only boxes."

They left the man still scratching his head. Jimmy Zest thought that maybe, if he stopped scratching, his hair wouldn't get loose and fall out.

Back home, his mum looked as if she meant business. Slap! Bang! Wallop! she went round his legs. Then she sent him up to his room.

The limping Jimmy Zest went up the stairs as if he had just been in a fight with a hairy great monster.

He set his collection of egg boxes out on his bed. He had forty-eight of the wonderful things, which wasn't bad going.

He had only been collecting for a week.

Monday was the next school day. Jimmy Zest could hardly wait for it. On Monday morning he sneaked out with his schoolbag on his back and a plastic bag in his hand.

There was a jigsaw in the bag. And a Teddy. And a Slinky toy that could walk down the stairs.

At break time the teacher left the room with a flask full of coffee under her arm. Jimmy Zest asked his friend Legweak to stand guard at the door. Then he set out his toys on the teacher's table and stood behind it.

"Roll up, roll up," he shouted.

He felt like a man at the market with one small stall.

"I'm selling these toys," he said to his friends.

Penny Brown was there; Mandy Taylor, too. And Knuckles and Shorty, the twins. A boy called Philip McGowan jumped eagerly down from the radiator as Jimmy Zest held up a box and gave it a rattle.

"This jigsaw has all its pieces but two. I'm selling it for two egg boxes."

Nobody seemed very interested. Knuckles said, "What use is a jigsaw with two bits lost?"

"What use are two egg boxes?" said Jimmy Zest, quick as a flash. He saw some heads nodding at that, so he picked up the Slinky.

"This Slinky — ten egg boxes."

"Ten!" declared Philip McGowan, otherwise known as Gowso.

"You want it for nothing?" Jimmy Zest snapped at Gowso. "It can walk down the stairs on its own, you know."

Mandy Taylor said, "Oh, I'd love a Slinky."

Now they were interested. He had them now.

"This Teddy — three egg boxes."

This caused a fuss.

"It's only got one leg."

"Come on now, Zesty."

"Where's its other eye?"

"Was it your great granny's?"

"How'd you like somebody to chew *your* ears off, Zesty?"

There was so much criticism of the Teddy that Jimmy Zest lowered its price.

"Okay. Seeing that it's not perfect — one egg box."

Penny Brown put her name down for the Teddy because, she said, she felt sorry for the poor little thing.

Word came from Legweak that the teacher was coming back. Jimmy Zest warned them to bring in the egg boxes tomorrow or they would get no toys.

On Wednesday night he set his collection out on the bed to count it.

There was not enough room for all the boxes on the bed.

Later that week Jimmy Zest took a walk round

the shops where he lived. The first shop was a butcher's. There was a sign on the door:

DOGS ENTER THIS SHOP
AT THEIR OWN RISK.

The sign was low down on the door, as if the butcher expected dogs to read it.

Jimmy Zest went in.

"Have you any egg boxes, Mr Buckley?"

Mr Buckley was standing behind a table with a thick, wooden top. Mr Buckley was cutting a lump of meat with a big knife.

He stopped to glare at Jimmy Zest.

"Have I any *what*?"

"Egg boxes."

Mr Buckley held up his knife. "What's that?"

"A big sharp knife."

"That's a butcher's knife," he roared. "I'm a *butcher*. I cut up pigs and cows."

Jimmy Zest turned away from the big red face above him. He pointed at a row of plucked chickens. "When I saw the chickens, I thought you might have eggs. And boxes, too, of course."

"Have you not heard," Mr Buckley said very nastily, "they don't lay eggs when they're dead. By the time they get to me, boy, their egg-laying days are well and truly over. Goodbye."

Jimmy Zest did not bother to try the vegetable shop, but the grocer's was just round the corner. The grocer had a sign in his window, too, but it was not meant for clever dogs to read. It was meant for Jimmy Zest and people like him.

It said:

SORRY — NO EGG BOXES.
PLEASE DON'T ASK.

Jimmy Zest was not stupid. He knew what was happening. People like Knuckles and Shorty and Penny Brown and Gowso had been here before him, trying to get egg boxes to bring into school to buy his toys. They were all at it, the copy-cats.

Egg boxes were getting scarce.

It was Friday, and Knuckles and Shorty were on their way to school. It was not their favourite place, so they were not in much of a hurry.

Shorty was carrying a bag full of egg boxes. Knuckles had his hands in his pockets. He never carried anything. He was ten minutes older than Shorty and pushed his brother around a bit.

They were talking about Jimmy Zest. "*Why* does he want them?" Knuckles was saying. "Why, why, why?"

"I'm not worried why he wants them," Shorty

said. "I got a toy crane off him yesterday. I just hope he keeps on wanting them, that's all."

But Knuckles had a worried look on his face. He didn't trust Jimmy Zest. Maybe there was money to be made out of egg boxes — or something.

Jimmy Zest's mum was cleaning out his room on Saturday morning. She was in a good mood, and very pleased with Jimmy.

"Not a toy in sight," she said to herself, "everything neat and tidy. Perhaps he's changed."

Even his silly egg boxes were neatly stacked away.

Then she began to wonder. His room usually looked as if the contents of a giant pocket had been emptied all over the floor.

Where *were* his toys?

They were not in the drawers. They were not in the wardrobe. Under his bed she found only egg boxes. It was all very peculiar, for it seemed that the only toys her son had to his name were a dartboard, an etch-a-sketch and a space-hopper out in the garage.

The phone rang. "Hello," she heard, "is that the mother of Jimmy Zest?"

She just *knew* it was trouble. She wished she

could say, "Sorry, wrong number," and put the phone down. But she had to admit it. "Yes, I'm his mother."

"I'm not complaining," the voice said. "I'm really not complaining at all, Mrs Zest, but . . . I thought you should know."

"What? What should I know?"

"Well, he's going round the houses asking people for egg boxes. And, you know, he's got a wheelbarrow with him."

As soon as he came through the door, Jimmy Zest knew that he was in bother. It always meant trouble when they stood together like that, side by side, his mum and dad.

His mum spoke first. "Where are your toys?"

"Not anywhere special."

"Where's that?"

"Not all in one place."

"*Where* are they?"

He had to tell. Sold. For egg boxes. To the boys in school. And a girl or two as well.

"Oh, my heavens," Jimmy's mum said. "He hasn't a toy left in the house."

Then an awful look came over her face. "Where's Teddy?"

"Sold."

His mum turned and buried her face in his dad's shoulder. "Oh no, he's gone and sold my Teddy. I've had him since I was a baby and they don't even *make* them like that any more."

His dad patted his mum on the back to comfort her. He looked a bit embarrassed by the whole thing, and a little curious, too.

"How much did you get for Teddy?" he asked.

"One egg box. It wasn't in very good condition, you know," said Jimmy Zest. His mum was going on as if the thing was brand new.

They ganged up on him then — once his mother had recovered from the shock. Since his parents failed to realise the importance of egg boxes, Jimmy Zest had to shift armful after armful from his bedroom to the garage.

It took him ages.

Knuckles and Shorty had a great weekend. They spent most of their time gathering up stuff for their bonfire, which was coming along very nicely. They had quite a few branches and quite a few rubber tyres. The bonfire was nearly ready.

The twins were experts on bonfires. They liked to have one every six weeks or so — if they could get the stuff to burn. Knuckles often said that if it wasn't for school they could easily have a bonfire every three weeks.

Their great weekend was brought to an end by school on Monday. They had a bad day. It started when the teacher asked them how their project was coming along.

Knuckles had to admit that he hadn't even started. Neither had Shorty.

The teacher was furious. "*Everybody* has started. Penny, what is your project?"

"Graveyards, Miss Quick."

"Jimmy Zest?"

"Dinosaurs, Miss."

"Mandy?"

"Foreign food, Miss Quick."

Miss Quick turned to the twins. "You see? How dare you tell me you haven't started. What are you interested in?"

"Bonfires, Miss."

This answer made the teacher blink. "What do mean, bonfires. Explain."

Knuckles explained that what he loved to do best in all the world was to build a bonfire. He and Shorty did it all the time in the field beside their house.

"Don't be silly," the teacher said, "you can't light a bonfire when you like. You must have a reason, like Guy Fawkes day."

"Shorty and me don't need a reason, Miss. When we gather up the stuff, we go ahead and burn it."

"Then the problem is solved," the teacher said. "You two will do your project on bonfires!"

At lunch-time the twins went looking for Jimmy Zest. They paid four egg boxes for a dart-board and seven for an etch-a-sketch.

Penny Brown saw them and came over for a chat.

"There are some things I don't like about Jimmy Zest," she said. "I admire him in some ways, of course, but he definitely has his bad points."

"What like?" Shorty asked her. He was very fond of Penny Brown.

"Well, he's a squirrel, a greedy squirrel of the human kind. He's got every egg box in the neighbourhood in his garage. Every last one. I think it's terrible."

Knuckles began to feel uncomfortable. Penny Brown was a clever girl. Did she think that Zesty was making money out of egg boxes?

"Who cares?" he said bravely. "I've got his etch-a-sketch."

"And I've got his dartboard," added Shorty.

Penny Brown waved a hand, as if to dismiss their foolish argument. "Last year, when we wanted to go hunting wasps, who had all the jam-jars? Huh? Zesty. You know that gorgeous hat he has, with one hundred and fifteen badges on it? You know the one? Where did he get the badges?"

Knuckles and Shorty hung their heads in shame.

"Yes," Penny Brown went on, "off you and me and Legweak. And what did he swap them for? Huh? The insides of toilet rolls. The stiff cardboard bit. He knew we would want them, because that was the week *Blue Peter* showed you how to make a home-made kaleidoscope."

Penny Brown paused. Shorty was already in a rage against Jimmy Zest. Knuckles had his hands out of his pockets, which was a bad sign for somebody.

"How many of us made a kaleidoscope out of our toilet roll insides?" Triumphantly, she waited. Knuckles smashed his fist against the bark of a tree and hurt himself as Penny Brown finished. "Nobody!"

There was a violent silence. If Jimmy Zest had walked into view at that moment, Shorty and Knuckles would have torn him apart.

"I think," said Penny, "that we should ask that greedy squirrel some questions."

They waited for him after school. Penny Brown was very firm with Knuckles and Shorty. "Now no nonsense," she said to them, as if they were her pet gorillas. "I don't want any rough stuff. Jimmy Zest is a civilised person. He's not *all* bad."

The civilised Jimmy Zest came walking out of school, swinging his plastic bag. Penny Brown, Knuckles and Shorty fell into step beside him.

"We think you're a genius, Zesty," said Penny. "Don't we, Knuckles? Don't we, Shorty?"

The twins looked a bit confused. They didn't see how a squirrel could become a genius just like that. Penny went on, "I see you've got something in your plastic bag. I wonder what?"

"Guess," said Jimmy Zest.

"Egg boxes."

"Right."

"Whose were they?"

"Shorty and Knuckles gave me some. And I got some off the craft teacher."

"You *are* a genius, Jimmy Zest," said Penny Brown. There was genuine admiration in her voice.

Then she said, "We think we have rights, you know. We want to know why you want all these egg boxes, don't we, Shorty? Don't we Knuckles? How many have you?"

"Nearly enough."

"Nearly enough to what?"

"Nearly enough to do."

Knuckles had heard enough to do him, too. "Listen," he said, "there's something funny going on. I want my egg boxes back."

Shorty added, "You can have your dartboard back. We've got no darts anyway, Knuckles and me."

"The darts are extra," said Jimmy Zest, "two egg boxes each."

Tempers were rising. Penny Brown stamped her foot.

"You're nothing but a human squirrel, Jimmy Zest. How can you be so unreasonable? We'll find out your secret, you know."

*

It was nearly half-past eight, and very dark. Penny Brown waited at the shops for Knuckles and Shorty.

Eventually they showed up, eating crisps out of one packet. Knuckles had his hands in his pockets and Shorty was feeding him crisps. "What kept you?" Penny raged at them. "I've been waiting for ages. It's not a summer's night, you know."

Shorty crumpled the crisp bag and stuck it in somebody's hedge.

"What's the hurry?" said Knuckles. "The later the better."

Penny Brown tapped her wrist. "Listen. You two might be able to run the streets till all hours, but *I* come from a respectable home. And I have to be in soon. So come on."

They went along the road as far as Jimmy Zest's house. Quietly, they tip-toed up his drive. They could hear his TV blaring as they went by. It was nice and dark round the back of his house.

"Go on!" Penny whispered to the boys. "Do your stuff."

The twins went prowling. Penny waited as they tried to find a way into the garage. She had every confidence in Shorty and Knuckles, for they were always talking about their grandfather who had been a cat burglar before the war. Until the police caught him.

Penny Brown was not too sure what a cat burglar did, but she knew it had nothing to do with stealing cats.

She felt awfully wicked. It was a terrible thing to break into somebody's garage, but it would be worth it just to see what Jimmy Zest was up to. It was his own fault for being such a squirrel. She couldn't wait to see his face in the morning when he found out that everybody knew his secret.

Anyway, they weren't going to actually *steal* anything, except a look.

The minutes passed. Knuckles and Shorty stood whispering together. Then they admitted it.

They couldn't find a way into the garage — not unless they broke a window.

Penny was not having any broken windows. "You snooks!" she raged quietly. "You told me that your grandfather was a cat burglar."

Knuckles was very offended by the scorn in her voice. "He was."

"Then it doesn't run in the family, does it?"

Suddenly, a light went on. Penny clapped a hand over her mouth. The light dazzled her.

Knuckles' hands came out of his pockets so fast that he almost ripped his trousers off. A man came running out and grabbed the twins before they could move.

"Got you! After my car, were you? We'll see about that. And you, girl, you stay where you are. I can be just as rough with girl thieves, make no mistake about that."

The man dragged them into his living room through his back door. The whole house seemed to be coming alive with noise and light.

Penny felt so ashamed. Jimmy Zest was there, in his pyjamas. He had blue pyjamas, with sharks all over them. He actually winked at her!

"Now then," the man said, "let's find out who you are."

Jimmy Zest looked at Penny and smiled. Then he lifted the phone. "Shall I give the police a buzz, dad?"

Penny started to cry. She couldn't help it. It was the shame of being caught in the company of people who were descended from cat burglars.

Then Shorty spoke. Penny really admired him for it.

"Certainly not," Shorty said. "You needn't call the police. It's us, Zesty. It's only old Knuckles and me:" Shorty looked up at Mr Zest as if he was his Sunday School teacher. "Don't worry, Mister, Zesty and us are mates."

That settled it. Mr Zest let them go. Penny explained how she was from a respectable home, she wasn't a burglar of any sort. She told Mr Zest that his son, Jimmy, had every egg box in the neighbourhood under lock and key and that all they were trying to do was take a *look* in the garage. They weren't going to *steal* anything.

Penny, Shorty and Knuckles walked down the drive of Jimmy Zest's house together. Penny stopped at the gate. There was something she simply had to say.

"Shorty," she said, "I admit it. I've underestimated you. You were wonderful tonight!"

Shorty, who was a bit slow, hadn't a clue what she was talking about. He said, "Would you like to come to our bonfire? It's the day after tomorrow. You could declare it open."

Now it was Penny's turn to be puzzled. "Declare what open?"

"Our bonfire. We could tie a big ribbon round it and you could cut it with scissors, the way they do with motorways and things."

Penny looked at Knuckles, then at her watch and saw that she must dash home.

Knuckles and Shorty headed down the road to see if they could beg, steal or borrow a hamburger from the chippie.

Ten minutes later, Knuckles and Shorty had a stroke of the most fantastic luck. They were coming back up the road sharing a hamburger between them when they saw Jimmy Zest's dad reversing his car out of his garage. The lights of the car lit up every corner inside the garage. In that second, Knuckles and Shorty saw Jimmy Zest's secret in all its glory.

He had built a monster in his garage — out of egg boxes!

The twins were very impressed by Jimmy Zest's monster. It seemed to go all the way up to the roof. It had a big ugly head and a long tail.

Shorty's eyes bulged. "Did you see that! What was that thing? A big dragon?"

Knuckles smiled, a nasty, curling-up-at-one-corner sort of a smile.

"That's no big dragon," he said craftily, "that's a ready-made egg box bonfire."

In school the next morning, Jimmy Zest walked up to the teacher with his dinosaur project in his hand.

"I was just wondering, Miss, what we're going

to be doing this morning."

"Maths."

Bad news.

"It's just that I had other plans. Would you mind if I got on with my dinosaur project?"

"I would mind, yes."

"You see, I've got a section to write on how Dimetrodon uses his fin to catch the heat of the sun."

"Dimetrodon will have to wait, then. You'll do what everyone else does, James Zest."

She called the roll, then. Shorty didn't answer to his name, and neither did Knuckles. Jimmy Zest wondered where they were.

Penny Brown spent the morning trying to keep out of Jimmy Zest's way. She still felt very embarrassed about last night. Then, at lunchtime, he suddenly appeared out of nowhere and sat down beside her.

She felt like Little Miss Muffet, when the spider came. What was she going to say to him about trying to break into his garage? All she could think of was how he had sharks all over his blue pyjamas.

"Hello, Penelope," said Jimmy Zest.

The snook. He always called her Penelope, not Penny like everybody else. She wondered what he wanted.

"Penelope, would you give me back Teddy?"

So that was it! He wanted his Teddy.

"You're not getting it. I bought it."

"Well, it's just that my mum cries every night. She misses him, Penelope."

Penny Brown turned right round to look at Jimmy Zest to see if he was lying.

"She doesn't. Does she?"

Jimmy Zest shook his head sadly.

"She worries."

"About a Teddy?"

"She worries about its health. You know how old it is, Penelope."

Penny Brown thought how it was a great pity that people didn't turn blue or something when they told lies. Then at least you would know.

She hardened her heart. "I wouldn't give it back for ten egg boxes."

Jimmy Zest looked a picture of misery. He got up as if his legs had suddenly grown old and weary. "Then write her a note, Penelope, and tell her Teddy's okay. She'll sleep better."

Penny's eyes narrowed to vicious points. "You really are mean, Zesty. Imagine selling your mum's Teddy. That's the meanest thing I ever heard of."

But she got no answer. Jimmy Zest had got

tired of listening to her and was running across the playground.

Shorty and Knuckles came into school in the afternoon. The teacher seemed disappointed to see them, for the class had been quiet all morning.

"Where were *you* this morning?" she asked Knuckles.

"I had a headache, Miss."

"How painful. And you?"

"I had a headache too, Miss."

The teacher took a deep breath. "That's fine, then. You have the same colour of hair, the same eyes, the same head, I suppose it's only right and proper that you should have the same headache. Go and sit down, you pair of absolute scoundrels."

Twice during the afternoon, Jimmy Zest caught Shorty and Knuckles looking over at him. Each time, they looked away and giggled.

Jimmy Zest got a funny feeling about those two. He began to fidget. Why did the twins keep looking at him? Where had they been all morning?

When the school bell rang for the end of classes, Jimmy Zest ran up the road and arrived at his garage with his mouth dry and his tongue hanging out to find that his worst fears were true.

His model dinosaur had gone!

The furious Jimmy Zest kicked his space hopper up and down the garage. "Knuckles and Shorty are going to die," he promised. His space hopper went booming into the tin door of the garage.

He ran into the house, but his mother was worse than useless. "It couldn't be gone, that big thing. Your father can hardly get his car into the garage for the size of it. Who would *want* it for goodness sake?" Then, "Is it really *gone*?"

It was gone, all right. Jimmy Zest threw his leg over his bike and started pedalling. That dinosaur was the finest thing he'd made in his whole life — his greatest triumph.

"Knuckles and Shorty are going to die!" he yelled out loud as he pedalled like fury down the road.

Then he stopped. He didn't know exactly where Knuckles and Shorty lived.

But he knew where Penelope Brown lived! And she was in it with them. He rode his bike through her gate, right into the middle of the front garden. He threw his bike down and left it with its front wheel spinning. "Come out, you thief. Come out, come out."

Just to make sure she knew he was there, he gave the bell of his bike a good ring.

Her mum appeared first. She put her head out of an upstairs window and looked down at him with great curiosity. Then Penelope Brown opened the front door.

"I suppose you're here to tell about last night," she said. "Well you needn't bother, you tell-tale tit. My mum's not in. Anyway, she wouldn't listen to you."

Penelope Brown's mother leaned out of the window even further, even more curious.

"And another thing," her daughter went on, "if you tell my mum about last night you'll never get the rotten Teddy back."

Above Penny Brown's head, her mum gave a little cough. "Ahem! What's this about last night?"

Penny Brown clapped a hand to her mouth so hard that she almost knocked her teeth out.

"Penelope! I think that person in the garden should come in for a cup of tea."

"I don't like tea," said that person in the garden, Jimmy Zest.

"Milk, then."

"I don't like milk either."

"Shame on you, all those cows doing their best. I'm not giving you lemonade to puff out your stomach."

Mrs Brown closed the window and came downstairs anyway.

Jimmy Zest told her that her daughter Penny was hanging around at night with known criminals. That made her forget about cows and their lovely milk. He also pointed out that Penelope Brown had helped to steal an eight foot model dinosaur out of his garage that very morning.

"I didn't, I didn't," said Penny. "I was in school, Zesty."

"That doesn't matter," said Jimmy Zest. "It was your plan."

Everybody was quiet, including Penny Brown's mum. She sat looking at Jimmy Zest with a funny expression on her face, as if she had found something absolutely new in life.

"Are you the one who collects egg boxes?"

"I was," said the miserable Jimmy Zest.

With her chin in her hands, Penny Brown sat wondering how she could convince Zesty that she had nothing to do with stealing his dinosaur. She had only wanted a *look* to find out his secret. If only he had told them he was making a model, that would have been enough.

Suddenly, she spoke. "Oh flute! I know what's happening. I know what they're going to do!"

"What?"

"They're going to burn it. Your dinosaur is in their bonfire. It's going to go up in smoke."

"How do you know?"

"I know. Shorty asked me to declare their bonfire open. I didn't know what to say."

"I never heard of anybody opening a bonfire," her mother said.

"Well that's it then," said Jimmy Zest.

It was always the same. When he was four, he built a monster sand castle on the beach. Donkeys came along and wrecked it. When he was six he made a paper dart six foot long. It got run over by a lorry in the street. And now, here was his greatest achievement, an eight foot dinosaur, about to go up in smoke. It was enough to make you sick.

Penny got up. "Come on, Zesty, we might be able to save it yet. I know where their bonfire is. I'll get my bike."

The field where Knuckles and Shorty held their bonfires was a remarkable sight. All over it, like gigantic black dots, could be seen the scorched earth where the twins had lit bonfires on other occasions.

"Look," said Penny.

There it was, on top of a pile of planks, branches, paper and rubber tyres — his dinosaur. They had taken it apart, of course. The tail was near the bottom. Jimmy Zest thought that it could be easily rescued. But the two big legs seemed to be well stuck in. And right at the top of the heap was the splendid head of Tyrannosaurus Rex.

Jimmy Zest felt as if a fire had been lit inside *him*.

"They're going to die," he muttered. "I'm going to rush them, now."

Penny told him not to be silly. She said they would give him black eyes and a bleeding nose.

"Listen, I've got a better idea. I think I know how to get your dinosaur back."

The next day, Penny walked home from school with Shorty. They talked about graveyards and dinosaurs. Shorty did some talking about bonfires.

Then Penny said, "I've got some planks in my garage. You could have them for your bonfire if you like. But it would take a strong person to lift them down."

"*I'm* a strong person," said Shorty. He bent his arm and pointed to his bicep. "Feel that."

Penny squeezed his arm with a finger and thumb.

"I think you would do," she said.

In her garage she pointed to a ledge near the roof. Up there her father had stored planks of wood.

"That's where you have to go, Shorty," she said, "but take off your shoes."

Shorty looked down at his feet. "My shoes? Why?"

"You're a cat burglar, aren't you? Your grandpa would have taken off *his* shoes."

Off came Shorty's shoes and up the ladder he went. He had odd socks on, probably because he and Knuckles weren't fussy about whose they put on in the morning.

Once Shorty was up on the ledge, Jimmy Zest crawled out from his hiding place under a work bench. He and Penny Brown stood looking up at their prisoner.

Slowly, it dawned on Shorty what had happened. He looked from one to the other, then at the ground, then at his socks. "What am I up here for?" he asked.

"You're a prisoner. We're going to exchange you for my egg box dinosaur."

"You mean I'm kidnapped?" Shorty sounded quite proud. Then he said, "I don't want to be kidnapped. I'll jump."

"I doubt it," said Penny. "If you do, you'll break your legs. Anyway, the door will be locked."

"You wait until Knuckles finds out about this, Zesty," Shorty warned.

They left Shorty up on the ledge and came out of the garage. Jimmy Zest kept an eye on Shorty through the window, just in case he did anything stupid.

Penny had the note already written.

> Knuckles, we've got Shorty. Give me back my dinosaur and we'll give you back Shorty.
>
> Jimmy Z.

An argument started about who was going to take the note. Jimmy Zest wanted to go, but Penny said he was stupid. "Knuckles will start a fight if you go. He'll pull you off your bike."

Jimmy Zest put up his hands. "Let him try. Just let him try."

"Look, Knuckles is far better than you at that

sort of thing. He does it every day. He'll probably not hit a girl."

It was agreed. Penny took the note. Jimmy Zest kept watching Shorty, who sat staring moodily at his feet as if it was their fault that he'd been kidnapped.

After about fifteen minutes Penny came back with a dirty mark under her eye. She got off her bike, looking serious.

"That snook Knuckles *does* hit girls. He's not civilised, Zesty."

Jimmy Zest was not in the least surprised. Knuckles was quite capable of hitting anything that moved.

"What did he say about the note?"

Penny shook her head. "He says we can keep Shorty all night for all *he* cares."

Jimmy Zest could hardly believe it. "He said that? About his brother? His *twin* brother?"

Penny nodded in agreement. "Doesn't it just make you despise him? I told him he was a dirty rat and that brothers are supposed to stick together. They even have the same headache, for goodness sake. Guess what he told me, Zesty?"

"I couldn't."

"He told me he'd stick me in his bonfire if I

didn't shut my big mouth — that's when I hit him a kick on the shin. And that's when he gave me this."

Penny pointed to a small bruise under her eye and, after a pause for some sympathy from Jimmy Zest, they went into the garage to tell Shorty the news.

Jimmy Zest carried over the ladder and said, "Okay, Shorty, you can go."

Down came Shorty with a grin on his face as he reached for his shoes. "Didn't I tell you? I told you Knuckles would sort you two out."

Penny gave him the bad news, that Knuckles didn't care about him one bit, he was only interested in that silly big bonfire of his.

Shorty stood still for a moment with his right shoe in his hand. "*What* did Knuckles say?"

"He said we could keep you all night for all he cares."

"He didn't say that. You're a liar."

Penny wagged a finger at him. "I'm not like you, Shorty Alexander, I don't tell lies."

The brain of Shorty did work, but it worked exceedingly slowly. "You mean they'd rather . . . Knuckles would rather . . . he'd rather keep all those egg boxes than *me*?"

At first, Shorty looked very miserable and very hurt. Then his face clouded over with anger. "Huh," he said.

It occurred to Jimmy Zest that maybe Penny and he were in a spot of bother.

But Shorty wasn't angry at them. "Listen, Zesty," he said, "nobody's going to let me get kidnapped. I'll help you get your big dragon back."

Shorty stayed in Penny Brown's house and had a very nice tea. Then they called for the ready-and-waiting Jimmy Zest and went off to rescue his dinosaur.

Shorty wanted to wait until after dark, but, as Jimmy Zest pointed out, they might be too late then. The bonfire might be lit. They were going to have to do the job in broad daylight.

They got down on their knees and sneaked through the long grass until they had almost reached the edge of the bonfire. Shorty stuck up his head to see who was about.

Nobody. The place was deserted.

"Come on," Shorty yelled, "quick. Before he sees us!"

In a fit of excitement, Jimmy Zest ran up the side of the bonfire and sank up to his waist in rubbish.

Shorty made it look easy. He was up the bonfire in no time, and brought the dinosaur head safely to the ground. Penny tried to carry the body away, but some of the egg boxes came loose as she pulled.

"Oh, Zesty, it's coming apart," she shouted.

The struggling Jimmy Zest fought to get out of the hole he was in.

"Never mind the egg boxes," he shouted, "get me out before Knuckles shows up."

It was Shorty who did the real work. While Jimmy Zest and Penny Brown pranced about the bonfire trying to keep their balance, he rescued two dinosaur legs as well as the head.

"Come on," he shouted, "leave that other bit. We'll have to come back for the rest."

When they came back for the rest, however, they got a surprise. Shorty climbed up the bonfire to get the body and at that moment, Knuckles appeared.

A few seconds passed before he realised what was happening. He stared at his bonfire, now much flatter than it had been, then at Shorty, who was standing with the last bit of the dinosaur in his hands.

Furiously, Knuckles pulled his hands out of his pockets. He had a box of matches.

"I'll fix you," he snarled as he put a match to his bonfire.

Shorty began to do a little dance. "Knuckles, it's me, Shorty. Put it out. Put it out."

By now the wind had begun to fan up a very satisfactory flame which ran up the side of the bonfire with an ominous crackling noise. Jimmy Zest shouted, "Drop the dinosaur, Shorty. Save yourself."

Even Knuckles seemed alarmed at what he had done, and shouted "Jump will you — jump!"

They needn't have worried. Perhaps it had something to do with the smoke going up his nose, but Shorty's brain worked like lightning. He threw the bit of dinosaur high into the air and came flying down the side of the bonfire so fast that his feet hardly seemed to touch it. He didn't even stop when he got to the bottom. He kept right on going, straight into his brother, flinging out wild punches and yelling like a mad thing, "Burn me up, would you," — wallop — "you'll not burn me up in a hurry," — wallop — "I'll ruin you," — wallop — "some brother!"

Knuckles, of course, defended himself, and did some walloping of his own. Jimmy Zest and Penny Brown picked up the last bit of dinosaur and made off with it at top speed.

After a while they stopped and looked back. The bonfire was still blazing away. And beside it, on the ground, Knuckles and Shorty were still at it hammer and tongs.

The following night Mrs Zest heard a knock at her front door. She thought it must be the milkman looking for his money. She went to the door with her purse in her hand.

It was a girl. She had a Teddy in her arms.

"I brought your Teddy back, Mrs Zest," she said, "Jimmy sold it to me for an egg box."

Mrs Zest took the Teddy and gave it a hug. "He's a bad rascal," she said about her son. "He had no business selling it. It's very good of you to give it back."

"We think he's a genius, Mrs Zest," she said.

Without any doubt, that Friday was one of the great days in the life of James Zest.

At half past eight in the morning he opened the garage door and wheeled it out into the light of day — his model dinosaur, eight foot high and every bit as long.

Such a sight! You had to admire that egg box wonder. The main body rested on a set of pram wheels and, to make it even easier to push, there was a small wheel on its tail. As it glided down the drive, higher than the highest hedge, it looked like something from the beginning of time.

To get it out onto the main road, Jimmy Zest had to stop the traffic. Shorty and Legweak, who had been invited to help, pulled on a rope, and Penny Brown pushed.

The dinosaur was on its way — to school.

The sight of an eight foot dinosaur on its way to

school was bound to attract a crowd. People came in all shapes and sizes, offering to help. "Want a hand, Zesty?" they shouted, and whether Zesty wanted a hand or not, he got plenty.

So many came that they formed a procession. The grocer came to the door of his shop to see it pass. So did Mr Buckley, the butcher. As people drove by in their cars they sounded their horns at the wonderful sight of a dinosaur sailing along in the middle of a crowd.

As the procession turned up the hill to the school a policeman on a motorcycle came by to see what all the fuss was about.

"What's going on here, then?" he wanted to know. "Where are you going with that there monster?"

Jimmy Zest stepped out of the crowd. "It's part of my dinosaur project, Sir. I'm taking it to school."

"Are you going to teach it to read?"

Jimmy Zest heard voices as he pushed.

"That's him in the brown jumper."

"There he goes, Jimmy Zest."

"It's an egg box wonder."

"That's our school genius, you know."

"Maybe we'll get a half day."

Jimmy Zest felt very proud. At the top of the hill he saw the headmaster and some of the teachers waiting for him.

The headmaster was very puzzled by the whole thing. Jimmy Zest could understand that perfectly.

"It's a surprise, Sir," he explained, "I'm giving it to the school — free."

"What the devil is it?" the headmaster asked, and gave a signal for the school bell to be rung. It was ten past nine already.

At break time, there wasn't a teacher to be seen about the school. They were all at a meeting in the headmaster's office.

The headmaster did the talking. "Well, this is an historic day, ladies and gentlemen of the staff. As I'm sure you know, James Zest has presented the school with a dinosaur."

There was a lot of laughter at this. Somebody asked, "It won't go through the door of a classroom. What are we going to do with it?"

Some of the suggestions were not very nice.

The headmaster said, "James Zest thinks it should go in the school canteen. He says it's a meat-eating dinosaur."

There was a lot more talk about Jimmy Zest's

egg box wonder, and a lot more laughter. But in the end they agreed to let it stand in a corner of the school canteen — for one week.

2
The Thing in Cricklewood-Holmsy's Garden

ONE day after school Penny Brown took a risk. She walked home with Knuckles and Shorty.

Knuckles was not like his brother. Shorty was tough, but he hardly ever hit people — only when he lost his temper, which wasn't often. Knuckles lost his temper all the time and hit people for no reason at all, especially Shorty. Only once before in her whole life had Penny Brown walked home with Knuckles, and she'd been a nervous wreck. He had tried to thumb a lift down the school hill in a *teacher*'s car, and had got them chased when he threw a tin of shandy into a woman's garden. She hoped that his behaviour would be better today.

They were talking about the holidays and where they were going to spend them. In Penny Brown's opinion, Spain sounded like a very boring place. The grown-ups only went there to lie on the beaches and let the sun drain every ounce of energy out of them. Shorty said Butlins must be a great place if what he'd heard was true — that it was free. When it came to his turn, Knuckles simply said, "Hong Kong."

"That's very far away, Knuckles," Penny Brown pointed out.

"All the same, it must be some place, that Hong Kong. Listen, you pick up any toy and turn it upside down and look at it and what do you see? 'Made in Hong Kong'. They can make anything over there."

"Mandy Taylor says she's going to Italy."

"I pity them," said Knuckles.

"Either Italy or Greece. She says the sun there would tan you to a crisp."

"Maybe they'll put her in salt and vinegar and eat her," said Knuckles hopefully. Mandy Taylor was not his favourite person. Then he started to pick a brick out of a stone wall.

Penny walked quickly ahead, thinking how this sort of thing showed exactly the difference between the twins: Shorty got up on walls and walked on them, but Knuckles picked out bricks and made them fall down.

Soon they came to a tall and very forbidding

wooden fence along the edge of the pavement. A thick laurel hedge peeped over the fence like an extra barrier, and this hedge, with the help of a few sycamore trees, threw the entire section of pavement into cool shadow. Over that fence was the very private garden of Mrs Cricklewood-Holmes.

Penny knew very little about Mrs Cricklewood-Holmes — only that she was very rich; and that she kept Doberman dogs; and that her son's picture had been in the paper a few years ago because he had a pet falcon. It was impossible to see into her garden because of the fence on all sides, and the sycamores were too high even for human monkeys like Knuckles to climb. Then Penny saw what she didn't want to see. Knuckles had found that one of the planks in the fence was swinging loose.

"Oh no, Knuckles," she said, "please don't go in there. Not Cricklewood-Holmsy's garden, she's a millionaire for goodness sake!"

She might as well have talked to the nearest lamp post, for Knuckles was not the sort to pass up the chance of a quick nose round a private garden, especially one owned by a millionaire. After a glance up and down the street he went in through the dark hole.

"Don't *you* go, Shorty," Penny said, but too late.

Shorty's voice reached her from the other side of the fence, saying, "It's okay, we're just looking for bonfire wood. We're not after her money."

With her mind made up not to get involved Penny began to walk on. Then she heard a couple of stifled yells, some scuffling, and the furious rustling of branches. Shorty and Knuckles came panicking through the hole in the fence and fell in a heap on the pavement.

Penny ran to help them, but they were in such a state that they didn't even see her. Shorty's eyes had grown huge, Knuckles opened and shut his mouth like a fish looking for water. Then they took off down the road at a speed which Penny could not possibly match.

Penny Brown took a long, hard look at the hole behind the swinging plank, and wondered whether she ought to go through it. She nearly did — until she looked to see where the twins had gone and found that they were already out of sight. She decided that it wasn't worth the risk when she would hear all about it tomorrow. Anyway — probably it was only a dog.

But Penny Brown was wrong. The Thing in

Cricklewood-Holmsy's garden was definitely not a dog.

That same evening, as Mrs Zest was trying to get her son James away from the television set and up to his bed, there was a knock at the front door. When she answered it there stood two boys with curly, red hair — the Alexander twins. They had a bag of chips with them. The smell of vinegar from the soggy paper made Mrs Zest wrinkle up her nose.

The one called Shorty spoke first. "Hello, Missus. Is Zesty coming out?"

"Hello, Shorty, I think you're the one I know. I take it this is your brother."

"Yeah, Knuckles. We've got news for Zesty."

"Oh? What's that?"

"Uh-uh. It's a secret."

"Well in that case I'll get James for you."

Between them, Knuckles and Shorty put together the story of what they'd seen in Cricklewood-Holmsy's garden: how the Thing appeared out of nowhere and stood on the grass looking all around it, "smelling the wind", as Shorty put it. It was so big, they said, that it couldn't get through Zesty's front door without bending double. And the head on it! That big black head with no eyes, no nose, no mouth. Shorty shuddered to think of it, then fed his face a chip.

"Was it a sort of phantom?" Jimmy Zest prompted.

"What's that?"

"Like a ghost. Something that wasn't there."

"It was there all right," said Knuckles, "big and straight and stiff, and with this big black head. It was Anti-human."

"Anti-human?"

"That's what I call it — the Anti-human."

"Was it carrying anything?"

"Certainly. It had a sort of a gun thing tucked in here, under its elbow."

"So it had arms?"

"And legs," said Shorty. "It walked from side to side like this," — he went on a tour of the hall — "as if it had no knees. I've never seen anything like it before, Zesty. It was like . . . like . . ."

"Anti-human," Knuckles finished gravely.

Jimmy Zest stood under the light in the hall looking thoughtful, as if he might have an idea what this Thing was.

"We'll take a look at it," he said.

"Now!" The terror flared in Shorty's eyes at the thought of seeing that monster in the gloom.

"No, not now. Someday after school."

As Knuckles left, he said very seriously, "Not a word, Zesty, not a word. This is secret."

Penny Brown sat beside the twins through dinners. It wasn't a nice experience, for neither Knuckles nor Shorty liked to waste time talking when there was food about. They shovelled potatoes into their mouths as if their elbows were mechanical diggers, and they were up for seconds before some people had sat down with their first course. Penny wondered whether the pair of them would come to school at all if it wasn't for the dinners.

She asked, for the third time, "What did you see in Cricklewood-Holmsy's garden?"

No answer came. Only the sound of them guzzling other people's left-over prunes.

Outside in the playground they were worse. Knuckles kept making quiet remarks about phantoms and spacemen and Anti-humans, and Shorty declared that the whole Earth might be in danger.

"What's the matter with you two?" Penny

demanded when she lost patience. "You're acting as if I'm not even here. Shorty, *you* tell me — what did you see in Cricklewood-Holmsy's garden? Bet it was only a snook of a dog."

Shorty looked at Knuckles, who said they might as well tell her if she swore never to pass the information to any other living human being. "Especially not Mandy Taylor," added Knuckles.

Penny Brown closed her eyes and swore.

"Well," Shorty began, "we saw a phantom, or a spaceman, we don't know which. Big gloves it had, and no face. I call it the Thing, Knuckles says it's Anti-human and the whole Earth could be in danger."

"Such rubbish," said Penny Brown.

Knuckles held up his left hand very seriously.

"You see that hand? I swear by my left hand that no human being should go into Cricklewood-Holmsy's garden alone."

"What's so special about your left hand?"

"All left hands are special, the veins go straight to your heart."

At that moment Jimmy Zest came around the corner with Gowso and Legweak. Penny rushed off to find Mandy Taylor so that they could talk over this latest piece of news before afternoon lessons.

Of course she'd promised not to tell. On the other hand, if there was evil in that garden, people ought to know about it for their own safety.

They were very solemn, and very quiet, as they stood before the swinging plank in the fence that guarded Cricklewood-Holmsy's garden. Nervously, Mandy Taylor twisted the thin gold ring on her little finger as she said, "Do you really think we ought to go in?"

Penny Brown touched the swinging plank and looked a little disappointed that it hadn't been fixed.

"I'll go in if you go in," she whispered.

"What'll we say if we're caught?"

"Say we lost our ball."

"Oh Penny, ought we to go in?"

They stood arguing on the pavement like a couple of cowards and finally squeezed through together.

They squatted in the bushes and peered through the laurel leaves. At first nothing stirred, only a startled bird or two. Mandy pointed to a row of tiny houses at the end of the garden, little wooden houses with roofs on, as if Cricklewood-Holmsy kept fairies at the bottom of her garden as well as Doberman dogs and falcons. Penny had no idea what the tiny houses were for, and very soon she didn't care — Cricklewood-Holmsy's phantom was coming down the path in broad daylight!

Mandy began to shake as it came closer to their hiding place. The big black head kept turning from side to side as if the Thing knew somebody was watching it. Something like a claw dug into Penny's upper arm and made her jerk with fear, but it was only Mandy taking a reassuring hold.

"Ohhh!" said Mandy Taylor.

Penny stood up as the creature paused. She'd seen a film once about these Anti-humans that landed from outer space and took over human bodies from their owners and, unless she was very much mistaken, they looked exactly like this Thing in Cricklewood-Holmsy's garden. As it fiddled with its gigantic gloves, Penny Brown wondered what kind of hands it must have.

"It's got a *green* gun!" she whispered hoarsely to Mandy, and got the shock of her life.

Mandy wasn't there.

Within seconds, neither was Penny. After a

dash to the fence she shot through the hole and saw Mandy waiting for her across the road. "Mandy, what *was* that monster?" said Penny Brown as they made their way home down the safer side of the street.

It was three-thirty the following day. A small group of people had gathered round the school gate and were talking fiercely among themselves, for the secret was out. There was something very peculiar about Cricklewood-Holmsy's garden.

"In my opinion," said Gowso, "it sounds like one of the Undead."

"Can't be," said Legweak.

"Could be," said Mandy Taylor, shivering. "A sort of walking corpse with its face eaten away by worms."

"Nope. Corpses only walk at night."

"Why's that?" asked Shorty.

"They can't stand the sun," explained Legweak.

Penny Brown's voice was not quite normal. "Yesterday was a cloudy day. There wasn't any sun!"

Legweak said he thought it sounded like a mechanical gardener with stiff legs — a sort of robot. Probably it clanked as it walked.

Knuckles turned to Jimmy Zest, who hadn't said much. "What do you think, Zesty?"

Jimmy Zest stood with his thumbs tucked comfortably under the straps of his old-fashioned schoolbag. "I think we should all go and take a look at it."

This idea was eagerly received by Legweak. "Then if it attacks us we can all jump on it. There's seven of us."

"Fair enough," said Knuckles responsibly. "Everybody stay together and do what I tell them." As the discoverer of the Anti-human he felt obliged to take charge. After a hard look at Gowso, who was known to cry easily, he added, "And we don't want any weaklings."

Then they all headed off to see the Thing in Cricklewood-Holmsy's garden.

One by one they disappeared through the hole in the fence, Knuckles first, and Shorty, then Mandy and Penny, Legweak and Gowso, and finally Jimmy Zest.

It was dark behind the fence, and cool beneath the shade of the huge leaves of sycamore. In a loud whisper Knuckles warned them not to leave the shelter of the laurel bushes or they would be seen and turned into a puff of smoke by the Anti-human's green weapon. They were a highly excited bunch of people hiding in the laurel bushes. Jimmy Zest sat on his schoolbag to wait for the action. Gowso climbed a tree and Mandy shrieked when Legweak tramped her hand into the dirt.

"Shhh!" Knuckles hissed.

Beyond the shadows of the bushes was a large, rectangular lawn all freshly mown and bathed in cloudy sunlight. The borders round the garden were thick with masses of shrubs and flowers. At the far end of the path, on a higher level than the lawn, stood the house itself. It had bulging bay windows on the ground and first floors. On the second floor many nooks and crannies had been built into the outer shell and there was even an interesting window in the roof. For observing the stars, Jimmy Zest guessed. No doubt about it, this was a very fine house. He could quite believe that Cricklewood-Holmes had a million pounds in the bank.

At the other end of the lawn the garden stopped at a wall grown over with creepers gone wild. Along the wall was a row of little houses with pointed roofs.

"Over there!" Knuckles whispered. They all looked to see where he was pointing.

Already the door of a small shed directly opposite them was opening, and nobody could deny that each heart began to beat a little faster at what emerged from it.

It came walking forward in the stiff and awkward manner of a medieval knight, with its

little green weapon firmly gripped in its enormous hands and with its great head looking too heavy by far for the shoulders that supported it.

Mandy Taylor got up on her knees. "Is it coming this way?"

"Sit still," said Legweak, who was trying to see over her head.

Penny Brown was on all fours. "I can't see its face, can you, Mandy?"

"No," said Gowso up the tree.

"It's *got* no face," Mandy declared in a horrified whisper. "How does it even breathe?"

Jimmy Zest heard scuffling and clattering in the branches above him and looked up in time to see Gowso making his escape along the arm of a sycamore tree and down on to the pavement outside. The Thing turned its triangular black face under a fantastic head-dress in the direction of the noise.

"It's seen us," Shorty shouted. "Run for it!"

As Mandy and Penny and Shorty went tearing for the hole in the fence, the creature began to shrill at them from the middle of the garden. By the time Jimmy Zest had gathered up his schoolbag and bolted after them he saw that it no longer mattered how much they hurried for they were all too late. A ferocious black Doberman was in the gap, baring its teeth at them.

All they could do was wait while the Thing from the garden came closer. Mandy, who was very emotional, began to yell and Legweak began to whimper. Knuckles picked up the biggest stick he could find and looked as if he wasn't going to give in to an Anti-human without a fight. Shorty tried to look stupid, as if he was only there because he'd taken a wrong turning. Penny Brown wished that she was Gowso and Jimmy Zest's mind was working overtime.

With one menacing arm, the Thing motioned them out of the shadows and on to the lawn. The dog came after them, at their heels.

Now they saw a strange sight. The figure reached up and pulled a black veil from her face. Mandy Taylor, when she saw the natural, silvery hair, allowed her lungs to collapse in a great sigh of relief.

"Oh, you're human!" Penny Brown said with quiet passion, and the stick in the hands of Knuckles dropped a little lower.

The woman was in a raging temper. "You children have no business being here. What are you doing trespassing on my property? Be quiet!" she yelled at Penny Brown, whose mouth had opened to speak. "This is a private garden — isn't that right, Caligula?"

The dog, hearing its name, echoed the anger of his mistress with a fearful growl.

"What are *you* doing, boy?" Mrs Cricklewood-Holmes yelled at Jimmy Zest.

Jimmy had his schoolbag open and was busy handing out bits of paper to Shorty and the others, who were standing in a rather dejected line. Then he reached into the inside pocket of his jacket, where he had a battery of fifteen clip-on pens and pencils of one sort and another. He made sure that they had one each.

"Mrs Cricklewood-Holmes, we are doing research for our class project on animals. I wonder if we might ask you some questions about your bees?"

Knuckles took his eyes off Caligula and stared at the equally unfamiliar sight of a fountain pen with real ink in his hand.

"My bees? What do you know about bees?" snapped Mrs Cricklewood-Holmes.

"Down there," Jimmy Zest pointed at the little wooden houses, "those are your hives. We thought that perhaps . . ."

Penny Brown gave a little cough. She saw what was happening.

"We're very interested, Mrs Cricklewood-Holmes. Do you get stung often?"

"Why do you think I wear all this

equipment? It keeps them off me when they start to buzz."

"The technical term is 'swarm', I believe," Jimmy Zest said. "I wonder what do you think of this new killer bee they've found in South America?"

"Killer bee my eye!"

Jimmy Zest leaned forward to look down the line. "Have you a question about bees, Shorty?"

"I dunno. How many has she?"

"What bees?" Knuckles said aggressively. "I can't see any bees."

In her prim and proper voice, Mandy Taylor asked sweetly: "How much honey do they give, Mrs Cricklewood-Holmes? We're awfully interested."

Mrs Cricklewood-Holmes seemed to like Mandy, the way all the teachers did. Perhaps it had something to do with her elocution classes.

"Well," she said, "I get enough to do me. But you people had no business coming in here."

"None at all," agreed Jimmy Zest.

"Don't come in here again."

"Never, Missus," said Shorty, still with an eye on Caligula.

"Caligula — away and lie down. Go on, away

and lie down. We'll let them go — *this* time."

She refused to let them through the fence, but led them up a concrete path, round the house and out through a side gate. Shorty was the last one through the gate, where he stopped to put a final question which had nothing to do with bees.

"Missus — is it true that you're a millionaire?"

Penny Brown sighed. Knuckles pricked up his ears, for he was very interested in the answer. Mrs Cricklewood-Holmes clipped Shorty on the head and said, "Listen, boy, there's more than you would like to know the answer to that. Now don't come back, for I warn you — Caligula never forgets a face!"

Outside on the street, the six classmates agreed that it must be their lucky day. As Jimmy Zest collected in his pencils and pens Knuckles said, "Hey — did any of you see her apple trees? She's got apple trees growing down in the far corner."

Penny Brown saw the gleam in his eye, and read the badness in his mind. "In the autumn," she said to Mandy Taylor on the way home, "he'll be back for those apples, you mark my words."

Mandy agreed. "I hope that big black dog's waiting for him," she said.

*

3
The Strong-Stomach Contest

IT was after school. Most of the teachers had gone home and the caretakers were busy in the classrooms with their buckets and brushes, getting the place tidy for the following day.

Miss Quick had not yet gone home. Neither had Nicholas Alexander. These two were discussing why Knuckles had not handed in a homework for two weeks.

"Even your brother Noel," said Miss Quick, talking quietly, "even Noel has handed in work to me. Now what's so special about you that *you* can be excused work which is attempted by everybody else?"

"I've been sick, Miss," said Knuckles.

"You have not been sick, you've been at school."

She didn't sound a bit angry with him. Some days she screeched at him and went red in the face so Knuckles figured that this must be one of her quiet days. Knuckles didn't understand teachers.

Miss Quick picked up her bag. "Well. I just

want to tell you that I'm getting rather tired of struggling with you. What will you do, Nicholas, if people simply stop caring what you do or what becomes of you?"

"Dunno, Miss."

And then she said he could go. Knuckles dashed through the school buildings and grounds and out into the street just in case he could see Legweak or Zesty to walk home with, but it was far too late, thanks to Miss Quick. Even the patrol man and his big lollipop had gone home.

Knuckles decided to take the long way home, past the supermarket and through Elm Street. From Elm Street it would be easy to cut across the golf course to his own house. With a little bit of luck, he was thinking, he might pick up an empty bottle or two near the supermarket — once he'd got a refund of fifty pence for returning a huge cider bottle, the kind with a pair of funny glass ears. What a find that had been! Poor old Shorty had spent the next fortnight trying to find one, too.

There were no bottles of any kind to be seen today. Instead Knuckles found only trouble. The minute he turned into Elm Street and saw Maurice Baimes with his mates, he knew he was in bother.

There were three of them. The boy leaning

against the gable of a house was Billy Parks. The one with the stick in his hand had a round body, round face and sticky-out ears. He was always called Gnome.

These two didn't worry Knuckles at all, for they were in his year at school. But Maurice Baimes was a different matter. He was older than Knuckles and had already left the primary school. Knuckles could remember as if it were yesterday the time he'd fought with Baimes in the playground during break. Neither of them had won because a teacher had come along and separated them. No doubt Baimes remembered, too.

"Forget your way home, Alexander?" he said. And he pushed himself off the gable wall in a very threatening way.

"I'm going through the golf course."

"No, you're not. That's our fence, *we* say who goes through it and who doesn't."

"Since when do you own the planet Earth, Baimes?"

"We'll let you through," said Baimes, "if you take a dead arm."

If you get hit hard enough in the right spot, your arm goes numb. Dead arm it's called. The thought of taking a dead arm from Baimes made Knuckles go hot with rage, but what else could he do? If he hit Baimes a smack on the mouth the three of them might start on him. On the other hand he had no intention of running away from them. People would soon get to hear about *that*.

Knuckles had bullied enough people to know that he had no choice. So he nodded his head once, and Baimes took him by the left arm.

"No," snapped Knuckles, "not that arm. Here." He held out his right one.

"What's the difference?" Billy Parks asked him.

"It's your blood. The veins in your left arm come straight out of your heart, ask any doctor. I'm not taking a dead left arm."

Left arm, right arm — it didn't matter one bit to Maurice Baimes. He closed his fist into a ball and hit Knuckles a paralysing thump. Billy Parks and Gnome sniggered with delight as Knuckles winced in pain. Then they let him go.

He ran for the fence which separated Elm Street from the golf course, slung his schoolbag over the barbed wire, and began to climb. From the safety of the other side he turned and yelled at the other three: "I'll be back for you, Baimes!" and away he went across the golf course like a wounded hare, thinking how this was all Miss Quick's fault, and how he would round up Gowso and Legweak and Shorty and anybody else who would come and then they would see who gave whom a dead arm!

In no time at all the news of this latest piece of trouble between Knuckles and Maurice Baimes had reached everybody's ears. Shorty flew round to Jimmy Zest's house and then to Penny Brown's and she phoned up Mandy Taylor immediately. Then Legweak and Gowso arrived on one bike to meet up with the others at the shops.

They wanted all the details, of course. Knuckles was eating chips, which explained why his mouth steamed as he talked. "We're going to go round and see Maurice Baimes," he said. "Nobody gives me a dead arm for nothing. Somebody has to keep an eye on Billy Parks and Gnome, that's what you're here for. Can you fight, Gowso? What about you, Zesty?"

"Fight?" said Jimmy Zest, as if this was a new word he'd come across. Knuckles punched the air. "Fight. With your fists, like that."

Nobody had ever seen Jimmy Zest fighting. There was a general feeling that his talents lay in other directions, such as making money out of things which other people threw away. He was the kind of person who got out of trouble by using his tongue rather than his fists. Once in a blue moon he got really mad — as when somebody stole his giant dinosaur — but as a rule he was not one for getting into fights.

Nevertheless, he made it clear that he did not intend to miss this one.

"I'll come too," he said.

They were ready. As soon as Legweak had fastened the lock round a wheel of his bike the group moved off in the direction of Elm Street. Then Knuckles noticed Mandy Taylor.

"Where do you think you're going?"

"Elm Street," she said, not too fiercely.

"Not with us, you're not."

"She is so," said Penny Brown.

Knuckles took a swipe at Mandy Taylor and made her run away a few yards.

"It's a free country, Nicholas Alexander," roared Penny Brown. "We can go if we want and we do want — don't we, Mandy?"

Mandy didn't seem too sure, but Penny Brown pulled her by the arm.

"Come on, we'll link arms and stand our ground. Shorty doesn't mind if we come, do you, Shorty?"

This was a bit embarrassing for Shorty. Mandy

Taylor had been a girlfriend of the dreadful Baimes and could therefore be called a bit of a traitor; on the other hand he did not like to offend Penny Brown . . .

It didn't matter. Impatient to be off, Knuckles was already striding away with Gowso and Legweak after him, then Jimmy Zest and Shorty. Bringing up the rear, at a safe distance and still with their arms linked, came the girls.

Their route took them past their school, which was all locked up for the night and completely deserted. Knuckles marched along at the front of his troops feeling like a general. It was a good thing that he couldn't hear what was being said about him at the very back.

"Look at him," said Penny Brown, "somebody should ring the zoo and tell them one of their cages is empty."

"I hope Maurice knocks his head in," whispered Mandy Taylor — which quite shocked Penny. Her friend was very polite and didn't often talk so roughly.

Then Mandy gave a little gasp as she and Penny turned into Elm Street and saw Maurice Baimes! Had he been expecting them? It seemed so. He was standing by a lamp post with Billy Parks and fat Gnome and he looked a bit angry, or, maybe, even worried.

"I'm not on my own now, Baimes," Knuckles shouted out. "Let's see how big you are now."

Shorty, who loved trouble better than his breakfast, shuffled with excitement as Baimes came forward. Gowso edged towards the back and Penny Brown noticed that Mandy did something very interesting. She moved away to the side as if she wasn't with Knuckles and his people at all.

Baimes took his hands out of his pockets. "Come on, then," he said to Knuckles.

"Come on yourself."

They stood glaring at one another. It seemed that the slightest movement would make one fly at the other.

"I don't think this is a very good idea," said a voice.

It belonged to Jimmy Zest, who stood there like a traffic warden talking to a naughty motorist. And Shorty wasn't a bit pleased with the interruption.

"What are you talking about, Zesty?"

"They're going to hurt each other, aren't they?"

"Well, it's a fight," Shorty pointed out.

"What's the sense in everybody ending up with black eyes? I've got a better idea. We should hold a strong-stomach contest."

This baffled everyone. Since nobody had a clue what he meant, Jimmy Zest went on, "Like a pie-eating contest, only instead of pies they have to eat something they don't like. Well . . . something revolting, actually. The one who eats most is the winner. It would be far more interesting."

There was almost complete silence. Somebody said "Flute" in the background and of course this was Penny Brown thinking out loud. Maurice Baimes appeared to be thinking over the idea and Knuckles asked, "What sort of stuff would we eat?"

"I'll pick the food," said Jimmy Zest. "It won't be very nice. In fact it will be horrible. It will take a very brave person to eat it. And there'll have to be rules, everybody can see that. I'll make the rules. We'll have the contest on Saturday morning on neutral ground. I suggest the golf course."

Shorty didn't like it, he was shaking his head. But the others were crowding round keenly. Mandy Taylor had gone right to the front — Penny suspected that she'd gone up there so that Maurice Baimes would speak to her.

"I'll do it if he will," said Baimes.

"Go on, Knuckles," shouted Gowso, and Penny Brown said, "You've got a good strong stomach, Knuckles."

She knew. She had watched him move mountains of food down his throat at dinner.

Knuckles grunted. "All right."

"Shall I make arrangements, then?" asked Jimmy Zest.

A frown had appeared on the brow of Billy Parks. "How can we trust you, you're on their side."

"Jimmy Zest is a very fair person," said Penny Brown indignantly. "He could easily be a lawyer or a judge, isn't that right, Mandy?"

"That's right," replied Mandy, sweetly.

Maurice Baimes looked long and hard at the impartial Jimmy Zest. Apparently reassured by what he saw, he nodded.

Jimmy Zest held up his hands to quieten the sudden buzz of excitement which had broken out.

"That's it, then," he declared officially, "Knuckles Alexander versus Maurice Baimes. There shall be a strong-stomach contest on the golf course — this Saturday morning."

But the next day was only Friday. They had a whole day to wait. And on Friday morning a row broke out between Penny Brown and Mandy Taylor. It was about the strong-stomach contest.

"You want Baimes to win," shouted Penny Brown, "I dare you to deny it. We all know he's your boyfriend."

Mandy Taylor blushed. "He isn't."

"He was."

"He's not. And I don't want him to win, I want . . . ," she had a problem now, for it was well known that she loathed Nicholas Alexander, ". . . I want it to be a draw."

"No chance," said Shorty, who knew what it was like to come up against Knuckles.

All the same Shorty became quite alarmed at dinner that Friday. Knuckles went up for seconds of apple crumble. Then he sent up a younger kid to fetch him thirds. In vain, Shorty tried to convince his twin that he ought to starve a little and so be ready for the big contest.

"Look," Knuckles told him, "this is only Friday. I've got to live in the meantime."

These small rows and minor worries were a sign that the strong-stomach contest had gripped the imagination of everyone who knew about it. And of course there was one big question which remained unanswered: what on earth would the contestants actually have to *eat*? Nobody knew but Jimmy Zest.

He disappeared at break time, just when everybody wanted to torment him with questions. At lunch time he was spotted up an oak tree and he flatly refused to come down, saying that he was writing out the rules for the competition and would they please go away and leave him alone. Penny Brown was raging at him.

Only guessing was left.

"I thought of frogs," said Gowso. "Think about frogs — they're slimy, fat and squelchy. Couldn't be better."

"Yuk," said Legweak, but Penny Brown was nodding.

"Zesty said it would be horrible. Frogs are horrible. I thought of scallops. Have you ever eaten scallops? They are *rotten*, they taste like crab's toes."

"Never knew they had feet," said Shorty.

"Ooh," Mandy Taylor shivered, "imagine eating crab's toes."

"Well, Mandy, you don't think he'll dish up chocolate éclairs."

This made Mandy Taylor smile. The more horrible the food, the more chance there was that

Nicholas Alexander would end up sick as a dog.

Ten minutes after the bell for the end of school, Jimmy Zest was jogging down Elm Street with some information in his pocket for Maurice Baimes. He had to wait a while since the secondary school got out twenty minutes later than the primary. It annoyed the methodical Jimmy Zest to have forgotten this, but he passed the time by studying the writing on the gable walls. The spelling of some of the words was wrong. He wondered whether people would pay him money to remove the writing. Methylated spirit might do the trick and it was cheap to buy. Then he heard someone saying his name. It was Maurice Baimes.

Jimmy Zest wasted no time in reaching into his pocket for a piece of paper.

"I have here the rules of the contest. Knuckles Alexander has already agreed to them. Would you like me to read them out?"

"Read away, Zesty."

"One. The contest shall begin at ten-thirty a.m. Two. The contest shall be held in the bunker behind the seventeenth hole."

At this point Billy Parks interrupted. "Where's that?"

"The pit with the sand in it — the one furthest away from the clubhouse. Three. The food shall be eaten in turns, first mouthful to be decided by the toss of a coin. Four. The food shall be eaten raw."

Gnome, when he heard that, stuck out his tongue as far as it would go. Jimmy Zest ignored him. "Five. The food shall be sufficiently revolting for this to be a genuine test of a strong stomach."

"Talk English, Zesty."

"Six. Flavoured drinks like orange etcetera shall not be permitted. Jimmy Zest shall inspect water bottles. Seven. Jimmy Zest shall be sole judge and umpire. Eight, and finally, the loser shall agree to take a dead arm from the winner."

The folded paper returned to Jimmy Zest's hip pocket. "Do you agree?"

Gnome had suddenly become very excited. "What'll the food be, tell us?"

"Can't say."

It was Baimes who objected. "Bet you've told Alexander."

"No. Anyway you're better not knowing, if I told you what you'll be eating you might be up all night, worrying."

This was a very good point. As Jimmy Zest headed off home Maurice Baimes was looking very thoughtful indeed.

*

It was a beautiful morning.

The sun shone out of a clear sky when the day of the contest dawned. By a quarter past ten Knuckles was leading his supporters into a stiff breeze blowing across the golf course. Gowso and Legweak came next with serious faces, then Shorty, and finally Penny Brown and Mandy Taylor, who had a woollen hat pulled down over her ears. She was busily complaining that her feet were getting wet with the dew.

"Well, you didn't have to come," Penny pointed out, rather harshly. She had a feeling at the back of her mind that Mandy might as well have stayed at home if she was only hoping for a draw.

Penny had another worry which she kept to herself. Jimmy Zest wasn't with them. What an awful thing it would be if the umpire didn't turn up.

She should have known better. The tactful Jimmy Zest, aware of the importance of his position, had decided that he ought to arrive by himself, before his friends, to show how fair he meant this contest to be.

And so, when the Alexander contingent arrived, they found Maurice Baimes already present with his supporters, and Jimmy Zest standing to one side tapping his watch.

"You're late," he said snappily.

"We were waiting for *you*, Zesty," said Penny Brown, just as snappily.

"I am the umpire," Jimmy Zest reminded her. "Water bottles, please."

Shorty and Gnome brought lemonade bottles to the umpire, who unscrewed each cap and tasted what was inside. Satisfied that it was only water, he jumped into the sandy bunker and set a plastic container at his feet. The label said Ice Cream, but every single person guessed that this was the food, and that the food was not ice cream.

Jimmy Zest said, "Before we start we need a look-out. I appoint Gowso to be the look-out."

"Aw, Zesty!"

There was no argument. The umpire, backed up by other voices, forced Gowso away from the bunker to watch out for early morning golfers.

Then Jimmy Zest flicked a coin, and stared hard at Maurice Baimes.

"Heads."

"Tails it is. Knuckles, do you want first mouthful or second?"

Knuckles jumped into the bunker and stared for a moment or two at the plastic container sitting in the sand. Through the plastic he could see the dark outline of a heap of things. He could almost swear he saw them moving. So he pointed at Maurice Baimes.

"Knuckles Alexander won the toss," called the umpire. "Maurice Baimes will go first." Jimmy Zest peeled the lid off the container.

The audience stared in silence. Then, "Oh flute . . . !"

"They'd make you sick just looking."

"He must have got those out of his garden."

"He's going to make them eat . . ."

"Worms," said Jimmy Zest.

Worms. A well-scrubbed mass of pink and brown creatures, each with its long, thin body curled under, round and over lots of other pink and brown bodies in the plastic container. Each worm was moving just a little, with the result that the horrible heap seemed to writhe and heave.

"Yuk, Yuk! They're bound to be poison," muttered Gowso. Even Jimmy Zest forgot to remind him that he was supposed to be keeping look-out.

"Every stomach has acids," said Jimmy Zest. "These acids will attack the worms and digest them."

The word 'cruelty' was spoken, which annoyed Shorty.

"It is not! Fishermen stick hooks through them all the time."

"Away and ring the RSPCA," said Legweak, which some people thought was a good joke.

Jimmy Zest was in a serious mood, and he warned the spectators that it was time to start. They retreated from the sand, leaving the two contestants alone with their umpire: and all three looked very solemn. After waiting for complete silence — which wasn't long coming — Jimmy Zest held out the plastic container to Maurice Baimes.

The boy from Elm Street picked a worm from the pile and held it dangling between a finger and thumb. He had a most peculiar expression on his face. It was as if the worm had a bad smell and he was trying to block up his nose by using the muscles on his face. The trapped worm curled, grew extra thin and pink, except for the end which bulged, and grew darker.

"Get it in your mouth, Mo," cried a single voice.

This was Gnome.

And Maurice Baimes did what he could to get the worm into his mouth. He swallowed his saliva and gulped and swallowed again and brought the worm to where it almost touched his teeth. Then he let it drop into the sand and walked away, saying, "I'm not eating that thing."

"Go on, Knuckles," cried a voice from the crowd.

This was Shorty, who knew that his twin must be hungry. Knuckles had skipped breakfast to be ready for this.

Without looking at what he was doing, Knuckles slid a worm from the heap in the plastic container. It seemed to go on forever as its body slipped through all the others it had been curled around.

"One worm to win it, Knuckles," shouted Gowso.

Shorty was sweating, so he took a swig from his brother's water bottle. Legweak spat into the grass as he imagined the worm slipping down his throat like a strand of slippery onion. Legweak hated onions.

With his eyes shut now, as if he was praying, Knuckles had the worm dangling above his open mouth. He suddenly let go.

"Flute! He's got it in!"

The eyeballs in Knuckles's head began to fly as

he tried to swallow. He began to hop about kicking up clouds of grit and uttering a sound like a dying man cleaning his teeth until, at last, he gave a panicking gulp, his body jerked forward and he gave a mighty retch.

Jimmy Zest, umpire, pointed at the second worm in the sand.

"He didn't swallow it!" yelled Baimes.

"I swallowed it, I swallowed it," screamed Knuckles — and bedlam occurred.

First of all, Billy Parks and Gnome pushed Gowso into the bunker when he declared that Knuckles had won it. Shorty clouted Gnome behind the knees and kicked sand in his eyes when he was down. Somebody passed Jimmy Zest with his hands up in the air as if he was signalling to an aeroplane pilot — this was Maurice Baimes calling "Draw! Draw!" And Baimes had Legweak talking to him, trying to explain that the worm had gone down into Knuckles's stomach and then come up again. "Here's the greenkeeper!" yelled Penny Brown.

By now the sand was flying. Shorty, on his knees, had managed to get hold of both worms and was claiming that his brother's definitely looked as though it had been attacked by stomach acids. Meanwhile Jimmy Zest was already on his way home, for he had realised some time ago that Penny Brown was right — it *was* the greenkeeper.

The greenkeeper was in a rage: "You bunch of . . . Look at the state of my sand, my bunker, you bunch of hooligan pests by all that's holy I'll sink my boot in the lot of you . . ."

The bunker was emptying fast. Shorty eluded a wild swipe from the greenkeeper's hand, which clouted Gnome instead. Mandy Taylor was standing there simply petrified by terror. All she could think of was how her daddy had belonged to the golf club until this moment. Now she would get him expelled.

"Run, you stupid!" yelled Knuckles as he passed her, running.

And Mandy ran too. She ran and ran until her lungs hurt, and she didn't stop running until she was absolutely certain that she'd escaped from the confusion which had put an end to the strong-stomach contest.

By Saturday afternoon Knuckles had become a bit of a hero. Even Mandy Taylor had to admit what a disgustingly brave thing it had been — to actually put a worm into your *mouth*.

They were all sitting on the wall at the shops, sucking ice lollies.

"You haven't said much, Zesty," said Penny Brown.

"Doesn't matter any more," came the reply.

"Oh, but it does matter, Zesty, we've all said what we think."

"And you were the umpire," Shorty added wisely.

Carefully, Jimmy Zest nipped the tip off his ice lolly with his front teeth.

"I'd like to know where you got all those worms," Gowso said.

"In my garden. You squirt washing-up liquid into the ground, that makes them come up. And

Knuckles didn't win."

Penny Brown stared round her, to make sure that Knuckles wasn't there to hear this. Fortunately he was away with Legweak pulling sticks out of hedges or something.

"He didn't swallow that worm," Jimmy Zest continued, "or if he did, he didn't keep it down. That doesn't prove he's got the strongest stomach — only that he can take a worm into his mouth. Sorry, Shorty."

Shorty didn't mind. He knew it didn't matter what the umpire thought: Mo Baimes was due a dead arm and he was going to get one, probably on Monday.

4

Legweak the Stuntman

ONE day in class Legweak turned red as a beetroot.

It happened when Miss Quick was handing back the homework books. "Now, I had one really excellent piece of writing this time," she said. "It was quite the best work I've received from this boy and I'm going to read it out."

Of course, nobody knew yet that she was talking about Legweak. Several people began to make guesses. Knuckles turned right round in his seat and said he'd bet ten pounds that it was Zesty. Shorty said from the back of the room he'd bet ten pounds that it wasn't Knuckles — which made Penny Brown giggle out loud.

This is what Miss Quick read out, 'My ambition is to be a stuntman in films or television. My dad thinks I'll change my mind but I've wanted to be a stuntman since last year. People don't realise that you have to work hard to make your ambitions come true. I practise every day on my bike. It's a very good bike. It's got hydraulic front suspension and four gears and dirt track tyres. I can jump three people when they are lying down. I think I could probably do six people if I had a proper ramp. That is my ambition.'

Even if Legweak hadn't turned the colour of a beetroot, they would all have known that this was bound to be his homework. Anybody who'd ever seen him on a bike had to admit that he had a lot of class.

"That was very good, Stephen," Miss Quick told him — she never called him Legweak —

"since yours was the best homework you can help me with the War Table today."

This made them all sit up. Even Knuckles tidied his desk and folded his arms like an angel. At the front of the classroom there was a table on which Miss Quick displayed objects of interest. She kept tadpoles there in the spring and in the autumn you could hardly see it for dead leaves. This table now had a label on it: OBJECTS FROM THE SECOND WORLD WAR.

Miss Quick asked Legweak to pick up an object from the War Table. He chose a knife with an enormous blade nearly half a metre long and with a dangerous point at one end.

"Careful, Stephen, it's a bayonet. If you were a soldier in the war you fitted this to your rifle and it became a kind of sword. Can you see why people talk about 'cold steel'?"

In the light coming through the window, the bayonet sparkled. Penny Brown shivered at the thought of it passing through a body.

"Was it pulled out of a dead German, Miss?" asked Knuckles.

Miss Quick sighed to hear this bloodthirsty question.

"No, Nicholas, it wasn't pulled out of anyone, I hope."

"Were you in the war, Miss?" asked a nice voice.

"I was just a little girl at school, Mandy, younger than you are. In those days we had brick shelters in the grounds of the school. Does anyone know why?"

Jimmy Zest's hand went up so quickly that he came slightly out of his seat. However, he was just beaten by Shorty, who answered, "For your bikes, Miss."

Jimmy Zest's hand stayed up. "To protect you from falling bombs, Miss."

"Yes. Although no bombs ever fell on us. Now let me remind you to ask your grandparents if they have any objects from the war which we could display on our table. We promise to take good care of them — don't we, Nicholas?"

They had Spanish meatballs for lunch. Knuckles told Mandy Taylor that when bull fighters killed the bulls in faraway Spain, the bulls weren't wasted: they were turned into meatballs and sent to the British Isles.

"Don't believe him, Mandy," warned Penny Brown, "he's just trying to sicken you so that he can get yours."

After lunch the boys drifted away to watch Legweak doing wheelies on his new bike. Penny and Mandy were not much interested in watching somebody riding around with one wheel in the air. A bike was a thing with two wheels and they could not see the point in making it go on just one. It was like being a human and having to hop around on one leg all the time.

They were more interested in the diagram which Jimmy Zest was scraping on the ground with a stick. "Enjoying yourself, Zesty?" asked Mandy Taylor.

She was ignored. Jimmy Zest added an arrow to his diagram in the dust and talked to Gowso. "If we had a ramp just there, the bike would take off into the air if Legweak was travelling at a good speed."

Gowso wasn't convinced. "There aren't any ramps like that round here, Zesty."

"We could build one. All we need are a few shovels and spades."

Gowso still wasn't convinced, but he whistled the others over to hear what they thought about this idea. Legweak got off his bike to peer closely at the ground.

"Where would we build this ramp?"

"The park after tea. I'll draw a plan and we can do it tonight."

The thought of actually doing the stunt made

Legweak ring the bell of his bike furiously, which got Gowso so excited that he yelled at the top of his voice: "Legweak's going to go for six people!"

Shorty swore it would be a world record.

And so, after tea, shovels and spades were taken up and carried to the park and, in a suitable place behind the bandstand, Jimmy Zest spread on the ground the plan he had drawn up for the construction of a ramp.

"Now," he said, pointing, "that thick line — that's the slope we're standing on. That shaded-in bit is what we're going to add on. That's the ramp. Legweak should be able to fly off it. Pile the soil in behind that plank."

He sounded most convincing. Nobody paid the slightest attention when Mandy Taylor asked if they had permission to go digging up the public park. Shorty had a bag of Liquorice All-Sorts with him which he now shared out, starting with Penny Brown and ending with Mandy Taylor: then they got stuck in. Jimmy Zest made them build a nice flat bit jutting out from the slope. They all stamped on the soil to make sure that it was firm. Then Jimmy Zest nodded to Legweak.

It was time for a trial run.

Legweak's new bike gleamed at the top of the slope. They could just see the determination on his face which was screwed up as if he found it painful to concentrate. The bike rocked to and fro.

"Vroom! Vroom!" said Gowso, making motor-bike noises. "Come on, Legweak — go!"

Up went Legweak on one pedal, and away. His hair streamed back from his forehead as he gathered speed down the slope and you could hardly see his feet the way they whizzed the pedals round.

"You'd wonder how he does it," said Penny Brown, "he's got legs like matchsticks."

At the last possible moment, as his front wheel hit the ramp, Legweak came out of his crouching position low in the saddle and threw his weight forward into space.

It was a disaster. The front wheel of his bike ploughed a furrow through the freshly dug earth and knocked the plank flat. The bike didn't get off the ground — but Legweak did. He performed a terrifying loop in the air and tumbled to the bottom of the slope where he lay absolutely still.

The first to react to this awful event was Penny Brown, who said "Oh flute!" and ran to see if Legweak was okay. Shorty came next. By the time Mandy Taylor arrived with Jimmy Zest, Legweak was up on his feet and hobbling back up the slope.

Shorty shoved a grubby bag under his nose. "Here, Legweak — take an All-Sort."

Legweak had no time for All-Sorts. His poor bike was lying across the destroyed ramp with its front wheel still spinning. It looked like a stricken insect. Legweak closed an eye and inspected the front wheel for a buckle.

"Seems to be all right," he said.

Now that the danger was over, everyone started to put their point of view. Mandy Taylor was first.

"I thought he was dead. What did you think when you saw him lying there, Penny?"

Shorty said, "If that hadn't been a trial run, just think, we'd all have been crushed."

Penny Brown put the same thought another way. "Oh very *good*, Zesty, Legweak did a world record *somersault*!"

The disconcerted Jimmy Zest stared humbly at the remains of his unsuccessful ramp, and shook his head forlornly as if here at last was something which he did not understand.

The attic in Jimmy Zest's house was reached by

way of a trap-door in the bathroom ceiling. His parents didn't allow him up the narrow home-made stairs on his own, so he had to ask their permission to go up and see if there was anything left over from the war.

His father took him through the trap-door just before bedtime. The sun had been beating down on the roof all day long, with the result that Jimmy Zest found it hard to breathe in the still and stifling air of the roof space. His father warned him to be careful with his feet — it was very easy up here to put a foot wrong and go through a ceiling.

While his father sat on the rafters smiling at old photographs, Jimmy Zest went on the prowl among the piles of junk — stuff like old furniture, old plates, huge and heavy old records. Every item seemed to belong to an earlier age and of course this made sense. Anything of any use wouldn't be stuck up here at the top of the house and out of the way.

He found an old-fashioned razor. "Ah-ah," his father snapped, "put that down, it would cut the fingers off you. Look over there beside the water tank and you'll see something from the war."

It was a big brass shell case, which his dad said

had been fired at the Battle of El Alamein. Jimmy Zest had never heard of that. Then his father told him to open a huge cardboard box if he wanted to see something interesting.

It was a heavy thing to lift. The thing in the box seemed almost as big as himself, and turned out to be a helmet of some kind, but made of rubber and canvas. On the front it had a panel of clear plastic stuff for a person inside to see out, and hanging down one side of it, like an elephant's trunk, was a floppy tube.

Jimmy Zest couldn't even guess what it was. "Put it on," his dad said.

The helmet came right over his shoulders and down to his waist. It was hard to breathe in there because the smell of the rubber caught in his nose. His father began to pump the elephant's trunk and on the inside Jimmy Zest could feel air blowing his hair about.

He took it off.

"Was it a gas-mask?"

"Yes. But this one is a bit different from the ones you usually see. It was for your mother."

This was puzzling, for Jimmy Zest knew that his mother had been born during the war. "You mean . . . this was for babies?"

His father explained. During an air raid or a gas attack you were supposed to put your baby into this helmet thing with its legs sticking out. Of course, it couldn't breathe in there, so somebody outside — the baby's mum or dad — had to pump the dangling trunk and give it air. The strong metal frame which made the mask so heavy protected the baby from damage.

Jimmy Zest found this a horrifying thing.

"Was mum ever put into that when she was small?" he asked as they came down the ladder.

His dad told him no, it wasn't ever needed.

The following afternoon this short note was passed round the class. It was signed by Jimmy Zest. Gowso read it first:

Another attempt at the world record tonight. After tea in the park. Pass it on.

Gowso shook his head as if to say, "Who are you kidding, Zesty?" but he passed the message on. Penny Brown also wrote a note and passed it round the class. It said that Jimmy Zest had a nerve to go risking Legweak's neck twice in two days.

But they all turned up after tea in the park, just to see what would happen. And *this* time, the others were not so easy to convince.

Jimmy Zest had a new diagram with him, which he spread out for them all to see.

"I know what went wrong," he said confidently, "the ground last time was too soft, that's all. This time we'll take the soil away instead of adding it on. See that shaded-in bit? We'll dig that out of the slope and make a ramp that way. This time Legweak'll be taking off from the slope itself. Do you see the difference?"

They saw the difference, certainly. But not one of them had any enthusiasm for this new plan — except Legweak, who could hardly wait to get going. After a few wheelies to warm up and some chat about which gear to put the bike into, he brought his machine to a halt at the top of the slope. The bike rocked to and fro, Legweak spat on both palms, and then he was suddenly away, raking down the slope with both feet whirling and his hair flowing in the wind.

When the bike left the ramp, Legweak stayed with it in the air. His machine and he hit the ground together — but they stayed upright, and after correcting a fierce wobble Legweak bounced back in the saddle and skilfully eased his machine into a sliding skid.

"Flute!" said Penny Brown, "he actually did it!"

A cheer broke out, Gowso yelled that they were home and dry as if *he* had been the one to make the jump, and Knuckles and Shorty took off in the wake of the victorious Legweak, who was riding about with one arm raised in a salute.

Now the excitement really began to mount. Everybody except Mandy Taylor agreed to lie down under the ramp and be jumped.

"But that ground's filthy," said Mandy Taylor.

"Mandy, you're not dressed for church," Penny Brown pointed out, "you've got your old clothes on, that's what they're *for*."

That settled that. Then they ran into a real problem, a giant-sized problem. None of them would volunteer to take the last place in the line. It was Shorty who pointed out that if Legweak's back wheel came down a bit short, you might get your ribs bashed in.

They stood in a group desperately trying to surmount this final obstacle. Gowso came up with an idea first.

"We could use a pillow for the last place. If Legweak jumps a bit short he'll just hit the pillow."

Mandy Taylor retorted, with great authority: "A pillow? Whose mother would allow a pillow out of its bedroom to take part in this carry-on?"

Knuckles suggested, "We could get one of those fake people out of a shop window. It wouldn't matter about his ribs."

"We could leave a space," said Jimmy Zest.

Legweak was almost crying with indignation. "What kind of a world record would *that* be? What would people say if I jumped over five people and a *space*? Or five people and a dummy out of a shop?"

Penny Brown didn't let him get away with that. "It's all right for you, Legweak. What if you landed on somebody's throat? They'd never speak again."

Nobody was taking any chances. What they needed was an incredibly silly and incredibly brave person to risk being smashed up by Legweak's new bike — and they didn't have one.

A gloomy silence fell over them all until Jimmy Zest spoke. He asked Legweak to lend him his bike.

"I'll be back in seven minutes," he said. "I'll do it — I'll take the last place in the line."

He was away for over ten minutes, actually; and

when he returned the others could hardly believe it was him. Across the park on Legweak's machine came this creature which looked as if it had just cycled in from the moon. All they could see of Jimmy Zest was his eyes staring out from the depths of the massive helmet with the metal frame.

Shorty walked round Zesty for a rear view of this monster, and saw some writing on the back.

"It says here 'Government Property'."

Jimmy Zest came out from under his headgear. "It was a gas-mask for babies during the war. My grandparents were supposed to hand it in but they didn't bother. If Legweak lands on this I won't get hurt."

Now they were all in business. First Shorty lay down in the line, then Knuckles. Once again Mandy Taylor threatened the operation when she said: "I'm not lying down beside *him*."

She meant Knuckles, so the twins changed places to let her be beside Shorty, the lesser of two evils. Then Penny Brown stretched herself out, and Gowso, then Jimmy Zest at the end of the line with his huge mask on.

There they lay, face down, six heads pointing to the north and twelve feet pointing south, waiting to be jumped by Legweak on a bike.

Mandy Taylor wriggled between Shorty and Penny Brown. "I feel like a sardine."

"You look like a sardine." This was Shorty.

"You smell like a sardine." This was Knuckles.

"If she's a sardine, Nicholas Alexander, you're a squid," snapped Penny Brown. "Hurry up Legweak and get this over with."

They couldn't hear him as they lay there waiting. The wind carried the sound of traffic from the direction of town. Then they heard the zing of Legweak's tyres in the short grass.

"Flute!" said Penny Brown. "Here he comes!"

She was thinking how this was what it must be like for insects when there were humans about.

She shut her eyes and tried to think of something else entirely when all of a sudden she heard a terrible clatter and an awful yell and her first thought was that Jimmy Zest had been chopped in two.

The line broke up in confusion. Jimmy Zest whipped his helmet off his head and knelt down beside Gowso to find out what was the matter with him.

"I . . . can't . . . get air," Gowso was saying. He had a panic-stricken expression on his face and his eyes bulged like ping-pong balls.

Legweak's jump had gone wrong. He hadn't even reached Jimmy Zest. The rear wheel had come down on Gowso's back and left a mark — as they saw when they rolled up his shirt to inspect him for damage. Already he had a sore, red bruise.

Soon, though, they had him sitting up and breathing more easily, and there was no need for the ambulance which Mandy Taylor had immediately called for. Shorty forced a brandy-ball into Gowso's mouth and within a minute he was up on his feet.

"That's the *last* time, Zesty," swore Penny Brown.

The miserable Legweak came over with the front lamp of his bike in his hands. It had broken off.

"Sorry about that, Gowso. I got nervous when I saw you all lying there. I fluffed it."

Gowso waved a hand as if it didn't matter.

But it did matter. Penny Brown, anxious to pin the blame for this shambles on as many people as possible, declared, "Yes. Well next time, Legweak, I advise you to jump pillows and leave people out of it."

5

Giant Money-boxes

JIMMY Zest was a born collector. He had collected egg boxes, badges, marbles, stamps, pebbles from the beach, key rings, comics, belemnites, things out of cereal packets — cereal packets too, the shells of dead crabs, penknives, model aircraft, books . . . and so on, and on, and on.

And when Jimmy Zest started collecting something, he went mad for it. He was at his worst one week in April just after he'd finished making a brand new money-box. To get money to put in it, he tortured his relatives and friends to give him jobs, charged young children 2p to see his puppet show and collected up money-back bottles. He would have gone so far as to play the mouth-organ in the street, cap in hand, if his mother had allowed him. He even thought up a scheme to get money out of his friends at school.

It began one Friday morning when Miss Quick left the classroom to go for her cup of coffee. She was no sooner out of the door than up went the lid of Jimmy Zest's desk, where he had stored a heap of stuff. He had a quarter of wine gums in there, a bag of balloons and a box of crackers left over from Christmas. He'd found them in the attic, in the battered old container where the Christmas decorations were kept.

Jimmy Zest called to the rest of the class, "Roll up, roll up. Get your April crackers here. April crackers on sale now, roll up!"

Penny Brown, Gowso, Knuckles, Shorty and the others were anxious to get out to play: but they had never heard of April crackers before. So they paused and looked at each other and wondered what Jimmy Zest was up to.

Gowso was one of the first to come over for a

closer look. Shorty came too, and Knuckles, who elbowed his way to the front for a good view. Mandy Taylor was careful not to stand too close to Knuckles. Legweak was right at the back when Jimmy Zest held up a yellow cracker for them all to see. "Get your April crackers here. Only one dozen left now, one dozen only."

"How much?" asked Gowso.

"5p."

"Your head's a marble, Zesty," Legweak pointed out, and another voice declared that they were no different from ordinary crackers.

The undismayed Jimmy Zest ignored the last speaker, who happened to be Penny Brown.

"Was it made in Hong Kong?" shouted Knuckles.

"They could be Hong Kong crackers," said Jimmy Zest, nodding his head. "With every April cracker you get a free balloon. That's a guarantee."

This news made Shorty twist round to see what somebody else thought of such generosity.

"*And* a free wine gum," said Jimmy Zest. "For just 5p you get a free balloon, a wine gum, and an April cracker."

Mandy Taylor said out loud, "You know, that's really good value," and the others believed her, for it was well known that Mandy Taylor did all the shopping in her house.

The April crackers began to sell. Gowso bought one, and Mandy, and when Shorty reached into his pocket for money, Knuckles went one better and bought two. Legweak called out in desperation, "Can I bring you my money after dinner, Zesty?"

Jimmy Zest took a note of his name and address.

Shorty Alexander and Jimmy Zest were walking down the hill after school when Penny Brown caught up with them. She enjoyed walking home with either one of these two. Shorty was always doing interesting things like kicking his schoolbag to death or making up rules never to walk on the cracks in the pavement. Zesty was different. He walked home with his schoolbag on his back and never *did* anything. What he *said* was often very interesting, though.

"How much money did you get for your April crackers, Zesty?" Penny asked.

"If you'd bought one I'd tell you, Penelope," came the reply.

"Huh. All I did was ask."

"I got 35p."

This brought a little nod from Shorty, who was a great admirer of Jimmy Zest's.

"Is it for a good cause or something?" Penny asked.

"Yes. It's for my giant money-box. I've got a money-box eight metres long."

Pennny Brown, always on the look-out for his tricks, said, "Zesty!"

Shorty was more trusting. "An eight metre, giant money-box! You're definitely a genius, Zesty."

Suddenly, Penny Brown stopped dead with her back to a lamp post. She took eight giant steps, and turned, and folded her arms.

"You must think we're stupid. Well we're not, are we, Shorty?"

"I am a bit," Shorty confessed frankly.

"Well *I'm* not stupid. A money-box from over there to over here! I get fed up with you sometimes."

Jimmy Zest stood with his hands up his blazer sleeves, like a Chinaman. "You didn't take big enough steps, Penelope. My money-box is longer than that."

Just for the moment, Penny Brown wasn't quite sure what to say. Jimmy Zest had created some great things in his lifetime, including the egg box dinosaur which had stood in the corner of the school canteen for a week. But an eight metre money-box . . . ? "Show us it, then!"

Ten minutes later the three of them stood on Jimmy Zest's doorstep. His mother said yes, they could come in if they took off their dirty feet. "She means 'shoes'," Jimmy Zest explained.

In they went. The money-box was a knobbly looking thing tucked into a corner at the foot of the stairs. Obviously it had been made from a mixture of cereal packet bits and egg boxes. A tube came out of the top of the box, and this tube ran up the stairs like a second bannister rail.

"Kitchen roll tubes," explained Jimmy Zest as he led the other two up the stairs. "Here, where the tube goes round the bend, it's not quite so good. Fifty pence pieces get stuck on the way down."

At the top of the stairs the tube of joined kitchen rolls ran up the wall and into the bedroom. And now, the maker of this marvellous thing took a handful of coins from his pocket and stood on a stool. "Listen," he said.

In dropped the coins. They rattled all the way

down and bedded into the other coins at the bottom of the tube with a quiet tinkle.

"Nearly eight metres, I've measured it. Have a go, Penelope."

"Give me a coin."

"I haven't any more."

Penny Brown fished out a fifty pence piece, the one she was going to use for Mandy's birthday present. In went the coin, down the tube, round the bend right to the bottom.

"You're a genius, Zesty," Shorty said again. "It's like a helter-skelter for your loose change. Who'd have thought of a giant money-box?"

"Come on," said Penny, "let's go down and get my 50p."

Up went Jimmy Zest's hand. A very serious expression came over his face. "Can't be done, Penelope." He sounded very sorry. "You can't muck about with a money-box like this one — this is the only way in."

Penny Brown was not the sort to kick up a fuss in somebody's else's house. On the other hand she didn't take too kindly to losing a whole fifty pence. So she whispered furiously, "What about my money?"

"You can have it back."

"When?"

"When I open the box."

"When's that?"

"When it's full."

"Zesty!"

"In about six months. You can see it's a very big money-box, Penelope. I'm doing my best to save."

Penny Brown struggled for the words to say what she was thinking. "But . . . six months! April-May-June . . . September! After the holidays. And what about Mandy's present?"

The sorrowful Jimmy Zest shrugged his shoulders in a hard-luck sort of way.

"You are money-mad, Jimmy Zest. You're a miser. You build great things like this just to *cheat* people, you're low, low, low, and you get up my nose!"

The lowly Jimmy Zest accepted this criticism calmly and offered Penny more April crackers out of a fresh box, but by this time they were out in the garden and it was war.

"No! You'll be sorry, you miser. You'll not get away with stealing other people's money."

"I'm only keeping it for six months, Penelope."

"*Kidnapping* people's money, then. Are you coming, Shorty?"

Shorty didn't know what to do, now that he was forced to take sides in the dispute. True, he admired Jimmy Zest; but on the other hand he was keen on Penny Brown, who was now storming down the road like a horse that had never heard of reins.

Shorty wandered off towards the shops, vowing to come home from school with his brother the next day.

In fact Shorty did not have to go to school the next day, for it was a Saturday. Even so, the news of Jimmy Zest's eight metre money-box spread rapidly among those who knew him. Gowso heard about it from Shorty while they were waiting to buy chips, and he told Legweak. And so, on Sunday afternoon, Legweak and Gowso went calling on Jimmy Zest to see the famous article for themselves.

As it happened, however, the Zest family was away for the day. Legweak had the good sense to poke open the letter-box of the front door to see what they could see.

They saw a blue carpet on the hall floor, a telephone-table-cum-seat, and a long thin mirror. Gowso, when he finally laid eyes on the money-box tucked away at the foot of the stairs, said it reminded him of a Norman castle with a stretched chimney. Legweak said it was a very good idea to build a giant money-box, but really, he thought he could do just as well himself with a little time and effort.

Both boys went home to plan their money-boxes.

Monday morning did not start well for Jimmy Zest. No sooner was he through the door of the classroom than he found Mandy Taylor and Penny Brown waiting for him — with a complaint.

First Penny Brown warned him that the girls in the class had agreed not to speak to him until he'd given back the fifty pence he'd kidnapped. Then Mandy Taylor waved a balloon under his nose and complained that the free balloon she'd got with her April cracker had a hole in it.

"That hole is supposed to be there, Amanda," Jimmy Zest explained. "It's the hole you blow through to make the balloon go up."

"Not *that* hole," snapped Mandy, "the balloon goes down when you blow it up."

"Then you mean it has *two* holes."

Jimmy Zest nodded his head as if this was indeed a disgrace.

"You're entitled to your money back, Amanda. Let me have everything back and you'll get a refund. Have you got your April cracker?"

After poking about in her schoolbag, Mandy produced one half of her exploded cracker.

"That's okay, Amanda," said the reasonable Jimmy Zest, "now your wine gum."

"I ate my wine gum."

"I'll accept it even if it's chewed up."

"I *swallowed* my wine gum."

"Sorry, no refunds," said Jimmy Zest as Miss Quick came into the room to start lessons.

And that was that. Penny Brown and Mandy Taylor nodded grimly to one another as if they meant business, and Mandy immediately swopped seats with Legweak to get away from the despicable Jimmy Zest. This meant that she had to sit beside Knuckles, who frightened her to death, but it was worth it. Knuckles was just plain bad, he was not a miser nor a cheat.

There was something different about Legweak this Monday morning. He had a giant brown paper parcel which he carried about with him. It was sitting by the side of his desk. Every now and then, when Miss Quick's back was turned, he hissed at Jimmy Zest and pointed down at the parcel and tried to whisper a message.

Miss Quick caught him at it. "Stephen Armstrong," — Armstrong was Legweak's real name — "what are you whispering about? And what have you got in that parcel that's so important?"

Legweak looked at her as if to say "I thought you'd never ask" and began to peel off the paper. Slowly, a most peculiar sight came into view. It was a dirty grey colour, and written over, so it seemed, by a thousand biros. Proudly, Legweak set it up on the desk for the truth to strike everybody.

"It's some kind of leg."

"Never."

"It *is* a leg."

"Then it's false."

"It's a plaster of Paris leg."

Legweak nodded at Mandy Taylor, who had guessed correctly.

"It was my cousin's, he had an accident playing football. Miss, he had two thousand signatures on that plaster. You can count them if you don't believe me."

There was suddenly a lot of wild speculation

about the false leg — until CLAP! went Miss Quick's hands, and back to their seats went those who had come creeping for a closer look. Then Miss Quick asked: "Stephen, *why* did you bring your cousin's plaster leg to school with you?"

"To show Philip and Zesty, Miss. It's a money-box, see? I stuck up the sides and closed over the top. The money goes in that hole."

"I see. Very good, Stephen. Now put it away like a good boy and show it to your friends at lunch time."

Legweak was as pleased as Punch at the success of his plaster money-box, especially when Jimmy Zest leaned over and congratulated him on a very fine effort indeed.

Penny Brown sat seething with anger all through the afternoon. Jimmy Zest never looked near her once, he sat doing algebra and getting his sums right while the rest of the class struggled with arithmetic, and all the while her fifty pence was lying at the bottom of his silly big money-box. It made her boil!

Which is why she and Mandy Taylor tackled him when they saw him and Gowso sitting on the school gates at the end of the school day.

"Right! Where's my 50p, Zesty?" Penny, with

her feet planted wide apart and her hands on her hips, was the very picture of determination. Gowso was on Zesty's side and spoiling for a fight with the two girls, but Jimmy Zest's head nodded in sympathy with Penny Brown as he took a crumpled piece of paper out of his pocket.

"I thought about it over the weekend, Penelope," he said sadly. "I don't feel good about having your money. Here."

The grubby piece of paper had a message on it.

I, JIMMY ZEST, owe PENELOPE BROWN the sum of fifty pence when my money-box is opened.

Penny stared at the message, then at the person who had printed it.

"This is no good to me. I want my money *now*. And so does Mandy. She wants her birthday present."

"I can't destroy my money-box."

"You're in big trouble, Jimmy Zest," Mandy Taylor joined in. "You're robbing two people, her and me. The police are just down the road, you know."

"I don't think they'd be bothered," said Jimmy Zest.

"Oh would they *not*? You dare come with us, then, and we'll see."

Mandy Taylor took off down the school hill with Penny Brown after her, running. They were followed after a short interval by Jimmy Zest and Gowso, who confidently declared that the girls were bluffing. After a quick march for five minutes, the four of them stood at the steps below the big heavy door of the police station.

"We're here," said Jimmy Zest.

"Go on, Penny," Mandy Taylor said indignantly, "you're in the right. Show him!"

Penny Brown looked rather doubtfully at the door of the police station. This was an awful mess that Mandy had got her into. She turned to Jimmy Zest to give him a last chance. Then, because she fancied that she saw a smile on that face, she ran up the steps and went right in.

Gowso began to fidget. "Come on, Zesty, time to go home." Pause. "*Home* time, Zesty, I said I wouldn't be late." Pause. "Will you come on?" And now, as the door of the police station began to open, "Cheerio, Zesty."

Away went Gowso at the run just as Penny Brown appeared in the company of a tall police sergeant.

"*Now* you're for it," whispered Mandy Taylor, giving the ring on her finger a twist.

Jimmy Zest waited as they came down the steps towards him, the policeman with his big black boots creaking. Shiny big boots. Penny Brown had her hands behind her back and was looking straight at the ground as the policeman pointed towards the town.

"It's not too easy if you don't know the town, love," the sergeant was saying, "but you go to the second set of traffic lights and turn left and that'll take you right to the place. It's a long road, mind."

"Thank you, Sir."

"Have a good time, now."

"Yes, Sir."

When the policeman went in again, Penny Brown spun on her heel to say vile things to Jimmy Zest, who had heard it all: but he was already on his way home, jogging.

"I couldn't say it," Penny confessed to Mandy, "my legs went to jelly when I got to the counter. Just you wait, Jimmy Zest," she called out to the diminishing figure in the distance, "I'll get you!"

Unable to bring the full weight of the law down on the head of James Zest, Penny had asked the way to the Museum, instead.

That evening after tea, when Penny Brown was out for a spin on her bike, she met Knuckles and Shorty near the shops. They were carrying a hefty log between them. When they saw Penny they set the log down and seemed glad of the rest.

"Where did you get it?" she asked them.

"It's a branch," said Shorty, "it fell off a tree."

Penny looked hard at the hatchet tucked into Knuckles's belt. Probably this was the trunk of a beautiful cherry tree from somebody's front garden. However, Penny had a problem of her own to talk about. She said how it was a crime and a shame that somebody could kidnap your money from April to September.

"It won't be worth fifty pence by then, Shorty. Inflation will have got to it and eaten it away."

Shorty shook his head wisely. "Inflation?" He didn't like the sound of it. "What's inflation?"

"A disease that affects money. Mandy thinks I should go to the police."

Knuckles, whose grandfather had been a cat burglar before the war, said that Mandy Taylor needed her head seen to. He and Shorty picked up their log and went marching home.

Two more giant money-boxes made their first

appearances in public the next morning. One belonged to Brian Parks, and his effort was much admired. His idea had been to turn an old television cabinet into a money-box by blocking up the screen hole with plywood. Then all it needed was a slit in the top to take the money.

The other effort was Gowso's. He brought in a wire budgie cage plastered with papier mâché and with a funnel coming out of the top instead of a slot. Legweak said that it might be rather easy to break into a thing made out of papier mâché. Gowso, who was not very good at taking criticism, snarled that it was a money-box and not a bank, and anyway, what was to stop you sticking a plaster of Paris leg under your arm and running away with it, money-box and all?

Later in the morning, when Miss Quick had the class nicely settled and the smell of school dinners was in the air, there was a very loud BANG! The teacher jumped about two feet in the air and whipped round from the blackboard to stare at the class with murder in her eyes. Knuckles had an innocent big grin all over his face. Beside him, crying her eyes out, was Mandy Taylor.

Four gigantic strides took Miss Quick down the aisle between the desks to the scene of the crime.

"Wha . . . wha . . . wha . . ." Mandy Taylor said as she breathed in with heaving great sobs.

Miss Quick ignored her and stood hovering over Knuckles like a cloud about to burst.

"What did you do?"

"Nothing, Miss."

"You did not do nothing."

"I didn't, Miss."

The remains of the grin were still there, for teachers did not easily frighten Knuckles. Miss Quick surrounded him with nice people like Mandy and Penny in the hope that they would keep him out of trouble and encourage him to do his work instead of talking about football and bonfires. "Nicholas Alexander, what did you *do* to her!"

From under his desk, Knuckles produced half of an exploded cracker.

"We only pulled an April cracker, Miss."

"He made me, he *made* me," Mandy wailed, "he said he'd put blots all over my page if I didn't pull the Hong Kong cracker with him."

Miss Quick nodded grimly, and knew that she'd heard the truth.

"I'll put blots all over *him*," she muttered. "Mandy, stop that crying for goodness sake." She turned to Knuckles. "What kind of cracker did you say?"

"An April cracker, Miss, made in Hong Kong."

The teacher took the remains of the cracker and examined it.

"Now you're trying to be funny. This is an ordinary Christmas cracker."

"No, Miss, that's an April cracker, I bought two from Zesty. He sells them cheap."

Penny Brown threw a wicked glance at Jimmy Zest, as if to say, "Now see what trouble you've got people into", then turned back to listen to Miss Quick warning Knuckles that if he let off any more Christmas crackers in April or any other month he would go home on crutches.

"And what's more," said Miss Quick, addressing the whole class and pointing at the papier mâché budgie cage, "no more money-boxes are to come into this classroom. I've seen three and three is plenty. Keep that sort of thing for your craft teacher. And now — take down your homework!"

The homework was a stinker — three whole pages of a story about a day on the beach. Penny Brown looked hard at Jimmy Zest to see if he felt guilty at everything that had happened, for every bit of it was his fault. But he didn't seem to be in the least concerned.

If Miss Quick thought she had seen the last of the giant money-boxes, she was mistaken. There was one more to come — the creation of the Alexander twins.

She was walking round the playground at lunch time, keeping an eye on things, when she saw Noel Alexander standing beside one of the long drain-pipes that ran from the roof of the school to the ground.

The boy had a cardboard box in his hand.

Gathered round him was a small gallery of interested spectators. As Miss Quick came closer she saw that the carton was an empty potato crisp box, and the boy had somehow fitted it over the mouth of the long pipe.

"Noel Alexander, what are you doing with that drain?"

Shorty turned and saw Miss Quick and knew he was done for. But he did his best. "I'm just standing here, Miss."

"Why are you holding that carton under that drain-pipe? What are you expecting to come down it? Gold?"

It was not a bad guess. The quiet, tinkling sound of something falling down the inside of the long pipe reached her ears. Miss Quick peered into the box and saw two coins, a one pence and a two pence. From some distance away, and from a great height, a voice began to call.

"What about that one, Shorteee? Did she come down?"

Shorty flashed a sick sort of grin at Miss Quick, who was rapidly putting one and one together and getting two. If Shorty Alexander was down here, then up there, on the roof, must be . . .

"Come down!" she screamed at the figure who

was suddenly trying to hide on the flat roof, "Nicholas Alexander, what are you doing up there?"

A red head appeared over the rim of the roof. "He's going to be a fireman when he grows up, Miss," Shorty said, as if that might make some difference. "If he ever grows up," snapped Miss Quick. "Do you hear me up there? Come down this instant!"

Now the foolish boy was lying on his stomach and calling down to her through cupped hands. Miss Quick had a horrible image of him falling through the air and crashing to the ground.

". . . Making . . . huge big long . . . box . . . like the one . . . Zesty has."

It didn't make any sense. Miss Quick turned to his brother for a translation. Shorty licked his lips unhappily.

"We're making a giant money-box, Miss."

"A what? A giant what?"

"Money-box, Miss."

"Out of a *drain-pipe*?"

Very gravely, Miss Quick drew herself to her full height and said, "You boys are mad. You twins are worse than bad, you realise that? You are mad. As hatters. What are you?" "Mad,

Miss," Shorty said obediently.

Miss Quick nodded, somewhat satisfied. "Yes. I can deal with badness, it's part of my job. But this is different. You will bring your mad brother to the staff room door if he comes down in one piece, and the three of us shall visit the headmaster. Understood?"

Shorty swallowed miserably.

That night, the patience of Mr Zest came to a sudden end when he almost broke his leg on the bottom stair. It happened when he tried to avoid trampling on the cluster of egg boxes, missed his footing, and fell. He called his son down from his bedroom, pointed at the offending box, and said, "Open up that thing with the tubes and get rid of it before it kills somebody."

Mrs Zest entered the conversation, grumbling. "I can't shut his bedroom door because of it. It's become a tourist attraction, did you know that? People actually come round to see it."

They were ganging up on him again, so Jimmy Zest obliged. When he counted his money, he found that after four weeks of hard effort he had accumulated the pathetic sum of £2.48. It was most disappointing, particularly since fifty pence of it belonged to somebody else.

Five minutes later, Penny Brown was called down from her bedroom, where she was reading about bees in an encyclopedia.

"Phone for you, Penny," her father said.

It wasn't Mandy, as she'd thought.

"I was thinking about you, Penelope," she heard him say, "about you and your fifty pence."

"Oh?" Penny said cautiously. This might well be another crooked fiddle.

"It's time you had your money back, Penelope. Six months is too long a time for you to wait. When is Amanda's birthday?"

"Saturday."

"I'll bring it into school tomorrow. Will that give you time to get her a present?"

"Actually I was just going to get her a packet of felt tips."

"Oh, very useful, Penelope."

This was unexpectedly decent behaviour from Jimmy Zest. Imagine him thinking about her like that.

Jimmy Zext had some very good points, after all. Penny had actually heard him congratulating Knuckles and Shirty on their

stupid drain-pipe money-box idea—he wasn't
a bit jealous of people.

Really, she liked Jimmy Zest quite a lot.

"Are you still there, Penelope?"

"Yes. See you tomorrow with my 50p,
Zesty, okay?"